FROM KNOWLEDGE
TO REVELATION

From Knowledge to Revelation:

My Testimony of God's Mercy and Grace

Cynthia Kay Elias, MN, MBA, DN, PhD

iUniverse, Inc.
New York   Bloomington

From Knowledge to Revelation:
My Testimony of God's Mercy and Grace

iUniverse books may be ordered through booksellers or by contacting:
iUniverse
1663 Liberty Drive
Bloomington, IN 47403
www.iuniverse.com
1-800-Authors (1-800-288-4677)

Because of the dynamic nature of the Internet, any Web addresses or links contained in this book may have changed since publication and may no longer be valid. The views expressed in this work are solely those of the author and do not necessarily reflect the views of the publisher, and the publisher hereby disclaims any responsibility for them.

ISBN: 978-1-4401-6219-0 (pbk)
ISBN: 978-1-4401-6220-6 (ebk)

Library of Congress Control Number: 2009934130

Printed in the United States of America
iUniverse rev. date: 9/24/2009

All Scripture quotations are taken from the authorized King James Version. All references are used by permission.

To my husband

Contents

Foreword

I was captured and carried away into Cynthia's world as I read her story. This is the story of the Lord's providential care for his children and his perfect oversight of their lives. It is the story of shame disappearing when God enlightens and delivers Cynthia from death, disappointment, and destruction. It is Cynthia's story of how the truth made her free. If ever you doubted the Lord's loving care and oversight of your life, Cynthia's story of grace will both strengthen and stir you. I have the privilege to be Cynthia's pastor, and I am the beneficiary of her infectious enthusiasm for life and her love for Abba Father!

Blessings,
Rev. John M. Raymer
Lead Pastor
Peace Tower Church
Ottawa, Ontario

Preface

In October 2004, I included a brief testimony in the very first e-mail sent to my sweetheart. I wanted George Elias to know how Jesus Christ transformed my life and how God inspired me to publish my testimony. George, a widower and preacher's kid who knew his Bible from cover to cover, asked me to marry him. Two years into our marriage, during my daily journaling, the Lord made it clear to write *From Knowledge to Revelation*. God revealed that sharing my testimony of how he transformed my life would affect millions. He can also transform your life. In April 2008, I wrote two Scriptures on my note board:

- "Being confident of this very thing, that he which hath begun a good work in you will perform it until the day of Jesus Christ" (Phil 1:6).

- "For he performeth the thing that is appointed for me: and many such things are with him." I praise God for the great work he accomplished in me" (Job 23:14).

I procrastinated in writing because I placed self ahead of others instead of sharing how Jesus transformed my life. Then, in June 2008, I came upon two additional Scriptures that helped me realize the writing and publication must occur now:

- "Oh that my words were now written! oh that they were printed in a book" (Job 19:23).

- "That I may publish with the voice of thanksgiving, and tell of all thy wondrous works" (Ps 26:7).

At that point, the opportunity came from the Lord to speak at a ladies' Bible study to share my entire testimony. This opportunity also verified that *From Knowledge to Revelation* must be written to acknowledge what Jesus Christ accomplished in my life. So, in obedience to the Holy Spirit, I now share this journey. This journey does not focus on my degrees, education, or knowledge. It is how God transformed my life of waywardness to a life of revelation and freedom as a prophetess. I wrote this book so you can have the same freedom.

Acknowledgments

I acknowledge the Holy Spirit, who supplied the words for *From Knowledge to Revelation*. I give special thanks to my husband, George Elias, for his loving support and the hours spent editing. His wisdom of the Word creates a home of peace, joy, revelation, and faith. God graced me with a righteous husband full of integrity. His search for God's truth through the Word has me where I am today. He is a faithful, godly man I could not do without. He is one who would sacrifice his own life for me. God delivered me, turned my life away from destruction, and gave me the gift of the best marriage in the world. Finally, I thank the publisher, iUniverse, for its part in the final editing.

Being confident of this very thing, that he which hath begun a good work in you will perform it until the day of Jesus Christ.

Phil 1:6

For he performeth the thing that is appointed for me: and many such things are with him.

Job 23:14

Oh that my words were now written! oh that they were printed in a book!

Job 19:23

That I may publish with the voice of thanksgiving, and tell of thy wondrous works.

Ps 26:7

He that dwelleth in the secret place of the most High shall abide under the shadow of the Almighty. I will say of the LORD, He is my refuge and my fortress: My God; in him will I trust. Surely he shall deliver thee from the snare of the fowler, and from the noisome pestilence. He shall cover thee with his feathers, and under his wings shalt thou trust: his truth shall be thy shield and buckler, Thou shall not be afraid for the terror by night; nor for the arrow that flieth by day; Nor for the pestilence that walketh in darkness; nor for the destruction that wasteth at noonday. A thousand shall fall at thy side, and ten thousand at thy right hand; but it shall not come nigh thee. Only with thine eyes shalt thou behold and see the reward of the wicked. Because thou has made the LORD, which is my refuge, even the most High, thy habitation; There shall no evil befall thee, neither shall any plague come nigh thy dwelling. For he shall give his angels charge over thee, to keep thee in all thy ways. They shall bear thee up in their hands, lest thou dash thy foot against a stone. Thou shalt tread upon the lion and the adder: the young lion and the dragon shalt thou trample under feet. Because he hath set his love upon me, therefore will I deliver him: I will set him on high, because he hath known my name. He shall call upon me, and I will answer him: I will be with him in trouble; I will deliver him, and honor him. With long life will I satisfy him, and shew him my salvation.

Ps 91

Blessed be God, even the Father of our Lord Jesus Christ, the Father of mercies, and the God of all comfort; Who comforteth us in all our tribulation, that we may be able to comfort them which are in any trouble, by the comfort wherewith we ourselves are comforted of God.

2 Cor 1:3–4

Introduction

Most information gives the promise of knowledge, but only the truth gives the revelation of the promise. One's life can come alive from knowledge. Knowledge dissemination comes in two forms: natural knowledge through head knowledge and spiritual knowledge through revelation. Most of us live by the world. Even Bible knowledge gained without any true impact on one's life results in an intellectual assent rather than a true encounter with the Lord. A person may know and quote beautiful insights of the Scriptures, yet fail to experience God personally in his or her life. Revelation acquired from the spiritual knowledge of God manifests in God's true and everlasting promises. A radical transformation occurs when one sees the revelation that takes one into a place of understanding God's power. Many agree to the baptism with the Holy Spirit, but fail to receive a revelation of the truth and life that exist through the word of God.

Spiritual truth can only be understood through spiritual renewal.

These truths of God become life. Revelation leads to a spiritual knowing. This spiritual knowing manifests beyond intellect and emotions, and travels into the realm of true faith. True revelation comes from God. Spending time in the Bible with prayer, praise, and meditation of the Word creates an environment for revelation. As revelation comes, heals, and boldly affirms authority in Christ Jesus, a victorious life emerges. Revelation knowledge opens boldness in a powerful agreement to receive God's truth. One obtains knowledge through teaching. But faith-filled words release revelation. Then these faith-filled words release the reality of the Holy Spirit. I discovered a way to explain revelation through the words of Watchman Nee in *The Release of the Spirit*:

> Revelation enables us to see what God sees. All things are laid naked and bare before Him. Any covering is upon our own eyes, not God's. When God opens our eyes that we may know the intent of our heart and the deepest thought within us in the measure that He Himself knows us, this is revelation. As soon as the light comes upon us we should immediately prostrate ourselves under His light and tell the Lord: Lord I accept Thy

sentence. I agree with Thy judgment. This will prepare us for more light.[1]

Revelation can take a few days or a few minutes; head knowledge can take years.

In the following testimony, I bare all that God cleansed. Also, God cleanses and effects a transformation for each person who gives him entrance. The manner and circumstances may occur differently, according to God's highest purpose for that individual. *From Knowledge to Revelation* is a book for every adult, including those who have gone through difficult circumstances, those whose lives are going well, and those with great knowledge and want more. There are three purposes in writing this book:

- To share the transformation of what God fulfilled in my life and what he can do for you

- For everyone to look at their life, praise God, and see his hand in all circumstances

- To experience God's love

This is done by having a personal relationship with Jesus, being baptized with water, and being baptized with the Holy Spirit. This experience releases peace, joy, love,

---

1 Watchman Nee, *Release of the Spirit* (Cloverdale, Indiana: Sure Foundation, 1965), 72–79.

and passion into one's life. Life does not promise a bed of roses, but one can experience peace, joy, love, passion, and God's mercy and grace in all circumstances. This creates a space for what really matters in life. The things that matter are loving relationships that are transparent and open. When dark secrets are revealed, bonds are broken, breaking forth into a life of freedom. This book reveals God's covenants and ways so one can come into or renew these covenants. May God's blessing abound as you read the words of this book.

Before I formed thee in the belly I knew thee; and before thou camest forth out of the womb I sanctified thee, and I ordained thee a prophet unto the nations.

Jer 1:5

CHAPTER ONE
BORN IN LOVE

This chapter reaches the spirit of the loved, the unlovable, different, and those wondering why a particular circumstance happened. This account portrays the everlasting love, mercy, and grace of God. I knitted John 15:16 into my heart:

> Ye have not chosen me, but I have chosen you,
> and ordained you, that ye should go and bring
> forth fruit, and that your fruit should remain: that
> whatsoever ye shall ask of the Father in my name,
> he may give it you.

Ephesians 1:4 also holds a special place in my being: "According as he hath chosen us in him before the foundation of the world, that we should be holy and without blame before him in love." The actual facts of my life resulted from knowledge, but the following testimony includes revelations given by God through thoughts, dreams, and visions.

Chosen by God

Mr. and Mrs. C. Quentin Martin of Lancaster, Pennsylvania, gave birth to a baby girl, Cynthia Kay, weighing six pounds and thirteen ounces. God creates each person special. My parents wanted a boy because they already had a girl. However, God designed three girls for my parents because perfection comes in the number three. God created me as the middle daughter.

God wants each person to realize that he creates each individual from a uniquely different DNA, sperm, and egg. I always remained a loving child. This came from God's love, which could not be quenched even in the midst of difficult circumstances. During those times, I failed to see God's presence until I received revelation from the Lord. The Lord said:

> I created you special and unique, as I do each individual. I created you from the foundation of the world. I sanctified and consecrated you before the creation in your mother's womb. I knew your every breath and every thought. I ordained a heavenly and everlasting relationship with me. I

created you petite and beautiful in my image and
oh so strong in will and spirit for my purposes
and plans. The gifts I bestowed eventually
blossomed into the fulfillment of my promise.
I created you petite for a special reason. I want
people to respond to you without intimidation.
Mother Teresa, only four-foot-eight, remained a
blessing to everyone. She fulfilled my work. You
being the same height, when they see your inner
beauty, they also see me. I also created an outer
beauty to show my love. I created you with Turner
syndrome so others would accept your calling.
I do things differently than the worldly ways. I
take the weak things of the world to confound the
wise. This is one of my ways.

Turner syndrome occurs when a female individual has
an X chromosome instead of an XX. One chromosome is
missing. Instead of forty-six, only forty-five chromosomes
form in the DNA structure. I share the following statistics
to give the full impact of what constitutes a miracle birth.
God creates each individual as a miracle, but, at times,
one can truly see the hand of God beyond what most
individuals consider as normal. Joanne Rovet says:

The results from standardized intelligence tests
reveal a mild lowering of full-scale IQ due to

3

performance IQs that are, on the average, 12–15 points below average verbal IQ, which is normally distributed.[2]

The average IQ ranges between ninety and one hundred and ten, but my IQ at age twelve, recorded as one hundred and thirty-five, in the superior intelligence range. In addition, the same article stated:

In the long term, fewer than 5 percent achieve higher professions, although some individuals with TS hold PhDs or become physicians or lawyers.[3]

I obtained my doctorate and PhD. Nevertheless, this merit remains in the realm of God's glory. God blessed me with few difficulties as well as a high IQ. I viewed myself as a petite woman who could not conceive children. In addition:

It has been estimated that as many as 99 percent conceptuses with 45 X result in fatal deaths within the first and second trimesters.[4]

---

2 Joanne Rovet, *Learning Disabilities Research and Practice* 1913 (1990), 133–145.
3 Joanne Rovet, *Learning Disabilities Research and Practice* 1913 (1990): 133–145.
4 E.B. Hook and D. Warburton, *Human Genetics* 64 (1983): 24–27.

The probability of a 45 X conceptus surviving to term is 0.3 percent.[5]

These statistics became available since my birth, along with the advent of amniocentesis, ultrasound, and other tests. God grieves for those who depend on tests to determine the effectiveness of an individual. Not only do abortions occur, but often at the expense of inaccurate prenatal testing. In the study by Claus Gravholt:

> Of 24 children who were born alive after prenatal diagnosis of possible Turner's Syndrome, 13 were karotyped postnatally, and diagnosis of Turner's Syndrome had to be revised for eight, seven being normal girls and one boy. This gives tentative predictive value of amniocentesis in diagnosing Turner's Syndrome of between 21--67 percent.[6]

This low percentage in proper diagnosis, 21–67 percent, constitutes inaccurate prenatal testing. In the same study, Claus Gravholt states, "About 75 percent of all fetuses with the syndrome are terminated legally in Denmark."[7]

This grieves God's heart, as it does mine. God chose each individual for a designed purpose. If one experienced

5 P.A. Jacobs and T.J. Hassold, *Advanced Genetics* 33 (1995): 101–133.
6 Claus Gravholt, *BMJ* 312 (1996): 16–21.
7 Claus Gravholt, *BMJ* 312 (1996): 16–21.

an abortion, one thing that shines a light comes from knowing God's everlasting love, mercy, and grace to be forgiven. The magnificence of God remains in the kingdom because of Adam's DNA. God's hand created everything. Out of the five million sperm, God chose me before the foundation of the world. God said:

> I am the potter who molds you into a beautiful vessel. I may take you through the fire. Perfection happens when I finish. I place you in the fire several times, place a glaze, and fire up the oven again. How beautiful you become. The DNA includes my will because I know the end from the beginning. I am the Alpha and Omega.

Early Signs of God's Direction

I praise the Lord for my miracle birth and my parents who loved me and wanted me in this world. My environment remained very loving and protective all those years until I married at the age of twenty. God created me with red hair and freckles. My mother would call my freckles "angel kisses" and would assure me that God created me small, beautiful, and special. God designs his inbred love of a mother to cover hurts that enter a child during these fragile years. God grieves when abuse happens to a child because these scars take longer to erase.

I enjoyed reading books, starting at the tender age

of four. I often read *Reader's Digest* on my uncle's lap. I usually presented a shy countenance. Nevertheless, my kindergarten teacher indicated I had hearing and visual difficulties and recommended glasses and a hearing aid. This opened up a whole new world. Afterwards, I blossomed as a beautiful olive tree. I no longer isolated myself. I could hear and see, and my intelligence flourished. I wore glasses and a hearing aid for one year. Then, miraculously, I did not require glasses or a hearing aid any longer.

Many earaches and sore throats occurred during my childhood. The Lord revealed to me that, to understand pain and empathize with others later in my nursing profession, I needed these experiences. At the age of five, the doctors removed my tonsils and adenoids. In the midst of the pain after surgery, I told my parents I wanted to be a nurse. With those words, my destiny to heal began.

As a child, I had a dream of marrying and bearing children. The dream flourished as I played with dolls. My father tried to interest my two sisters and me in hunting, fishing, and golfing, to no avail. He so wanted to share these things with his three girls. But God brought that love of sharing sports to my father when his two grandsons arrived. This vision of marriage and children happened, but differently than expected. I expected the Cinderella marriage with two children and the house with the picket fence. However, compared to my plans, God's plans far exceeded my vision. I am now married to the most godly man I know. I have seven children by marriage. God blessed me sevenfold.

The gift of dependability grew as I started babysitting at the age of ten. My parents encouraged me to save all the money I earned. By the time I turned twenty, I had saved $3,000. This dependability provided a pathway to excellent job opportunities and work ethic in my nursing and entrepreneurial career.

Small, but God's Perfection

Prior to entering my teen years, my parents took me to Johns Hopkins Hospital for testing to determine the cause of my short stature. I encountered many long and embarrassing tests. I started on growth hormones after the doctors diagnosed me with Turner syndrome. The difficulty with peer interaction began when other children made fun of me after the two-week hospitalization for testing. Despite the reaction from my peers, God sees perfection because he created me in his image. One of my favorite Scriptures to remind me to praise the Lord for exactly how he created me is Ps 139:14, "I will praise thee; for I am fearfully and wonderfully made: marvelous are thy works; and that my soul knoweth right well."

At the age of fifteen, the doctors stopped the growth hormones and placed me on estrogen to develop into a young adult. Jesus uses the weak things of the world to confound the wise. Yes, there existed a high IQ and cuteness according to others. However, in terms of the world's views, I did not fit the norm with my short stature. I knew God created me for a purpose, not to look up to man, but to look up to God.

God's Sevenfold Blessing

At this same time, the doctors told me that I could not bear children biologically. The shock appeared evident. I could not speak or express the hurt. I felt so empty. All of my dreams appeared shattered. But truth overshadowed the lies of the enemy. God showed me he had me in his loving arms. I could adopt. God had a different plan. Where love abounds, one draws on those motherly instincts. I did not understand the principle of empowering spiritual children at that time until God revealed I could give love to other children by teaching them truth. One truth opened to me when I realized God chose for me not to bear children physically, but blessed me sevenfold with my husband's children. Then I knew he called me to a larger family. God purposely placed the dream of children in my heart as a little girl. Only God brings gain from loss and makes me more fruitful in barrenness. I fell in love with Christ and wanted children in his image. That's when I realized I could be a spiritual mother raising spiritual sons and daughters who looked just like their Father God. Could anything be more important? God said:

> The blessing of spiritual children remains. Then I revealed the blessing of Jacob and Deborah to be part of your calling. Shock arose when you found out you could not bear physical children, but my plans are higher than yours are. I know the beginning and the end from the foundation of the world. I gave you a special instinct to be a mother. This motherly instinct will always be there. Give this to Jacob and Deborah, your seven children, eighteen grandchildren, and fifteen great-grandchildren. That is why I created everyone different. The ones who are physically barren will not be barren in spirit. Although, the option of adoption remained, I chose that you not adopt because of the circumstances that happened during those twenty-six years. I grieve at the abortions completed every day, especially in the United States and Canada. My nations need to turn and repent, and I forgive.

I do the same for individuals. No guilt remains if one had an abortion. When one repents, I forgive, and I always keep their children safe in my arms. I love my children even though I anger at their disobedience. I open up blessings when repentance prevails, and I renew all things.

God's Covenant of Salvation

At the age of fourteen, I took confirmation instruction at church. A formal acceptance of Jesus as Savior followed. This confirmed what comes out of my mouth is what counts. Romans 10:9 says, "That if thou shalt confess with thy mouth the Lord Jesus, and shalt believe in thine heart that God hath raised him from the dead, thou shalt be saved." Though I did this in ignorance, yet out of the innocence of my heart, I believed what I was saying. God accepted that. I did not enter into a personal relationship with Jesus, although I accepted Jesus as Savior. I thought he existed far away in heaven. I did not realize that he reigns within. God's presence continued as I sang in the church choir.

Kept Alive for a High Calling

While riding my bicycle at the age of fifteen, I collided with a car and almost died. God sent a protecting angel to intervene, keeping me alive. I remember a white flash prior to being thrown eight feet in the air. God protected me for my calling. The doctors performed an exploratory surgery, repairing a torn liver and broken left leg. Many strangers and friends prayed and sent numerous cards. I failed to realize how the power of intercession and power of prayer for the healing would decrease the recuperation time. My father's co-workers gave blood because I lost several pints due to the internal bleeding. I realize now that they gave the gift of life.

During the same time, I had a steady boyfriend, a childhood sweetheart since fourth grade. During the immediate recuperation that summer, my boyfriend broke up with me. I could not use crutches until a week before I started back to school. From July until I started back to school in September, I used a wheelchair to move about. The confinement and loss of my boyfriend caused a devastating time for both my mother and me. When he broke off the relationship, he stated I would find a greater love. The truth of those words came to pass. I not only found my first love, Jesus, again at the age of forty-six, but, at the age of fifty-one, I found the husband who loves me and waters me with the word of God daily.

In the last three years, God revealed these words to me, "I protected you under the umbrella of your parents. I kept you alive when you almost died in the accident, but an angel protected you for your high calling." God placed his hand on me for a high calling before the foundation of the world. Satan tried to deflect that plan, but Jesus always remains victorious. My strength increased through this process.

Preparation for a Healing Profession

During the last two years of high school, I had limited peer interaction and concentrated on my studies instead. I pursued the academic world to prepare for the task of entering college and pursuing a nursing career. The summer after high school, I worked as a nursing assistant, caring for eighteen residents. This prepared me for my future nursing career and started my true dedication throughout my profession.

God's Foundation Laid

This time would be the beginning of an era to prove myself to the world by receiving multiple degrees. However, the knowledge gained in all my years of education does not compare to the revelation God brought forth in my life, as shown in Phil 3:8, "Yea doubtless, and I count all things but loss for the excellency of the knowledge of Christ Jesus my Lord: for whom I have suffered the loss of all things, and do count them but dung, that I may win Christ."

God shared with me that the high school degree, the

smallest of my diplomas, is the foundation that takes the longest period of time to complete. That principle remains the same with Christian living. God's plan lays the Christian foundation during the eighteen years with one's parents. God also revealed to me:

> For if the foundation is laid, then the children
> will not depart from it as they grow older. They
> may go away, but I have their hairs numbered,
> and they cannot leave the flock. Once they have
> accepted me as their Savior, I woo them back.
> I wish that not one perish. I create free will,
> but, at times, one may choose to totally reject
> me. During these times, I grieve and shed tears
> because they fail to see my love.

God's Timing

Immediately after high school graduation, I attended York Nursing School, but I did not complete the coursework because God had other plans. God wanted me to complete licensed practical nurse (LPN) training. This upset me because I wanted my registered nurse (RN) degree. My mother called and enrolled me in the LPN program. I proceeded to go full steam ahead, earning excellent grades. This foundation started a great nursing career because I received practical training four days a week in the hospital. Nursing took a different turn as the years progressed. During the early years of my nursing career, I spoke with the patients, got to know them, ministered to them, and administered relaxing back rubs. Today, time constraints and new technology has largely discontinued these healing practices. I graduated from the LPN program, taking a position in a large four-hundred-bed nursing facility.

Cinderella Marriage

During this time, I traveled by bus alone to Virginia to visit a fellow high school classmate. We talked about the possibility of marriage. After several days, I pursued the possibility of a job and apartment in Virginia. My fiancé asked me to go to Baltimore to marry him. I agreed, and we started on the journey. Then, halfway through the trip, he decided not to marry me and sent me back on the bus to Pennsylvania. I cried the entire way home. It was better to find that out rather than to be unhappily married, alone a few states away from my parents. A year later, I met my first husband, and we dated nine months prior to marriage. Then, at the age of twenty, my "Cinderella marriage" began.

Let no man deceive himself. If any man among you seemeth to be wise in this world, let him become a fool, that he may be wise.

1 Cor 3:18

CHAPTER TWO
GONE PRODIGAL

Unequally Yoked

This marriage, one of my dreams since childhood, started unequally yoked, although at that time I did not realize the extent of what that meant. When one marries unequally, one comes out from under God's protective umbrella. I Corinthians 7:13-14 explains, "And a woman which hath an husband that believeth not, and if he be pleased to dwell with her, let her not leave him." I lacked the strength, knowledge, or revelation to then realize I needed to be a praying wife. Otherwise, wiser decisions would have set precedent. The Cinderella marriage I expected disappeared and was replaced with unspeakable physical and verbal abuse. I only knew love from my parents, and I did not understand the hurt I experienced. In 2009, the Lord revealed, "Weep not for yourself. Weep for the person who hurt you because he has been deeply hurt. Pray for him. I heal his hurts as I do yours. When you pray for others, this stops the cycle of hurt and abuse, allowing your healing."

Release of Forgiveness

It goes both ways in a marriage with respecting one's husband and the husband loving his wife. The other aspect is unconditional love, where one does not expect the other person to perform in a certain way. In the midst of all this, God placed his loving arms around me, and ministering angels surrounded me. I eventually realized that I needed to forgive my husband. After the release of forgiveness, God covered me with his mercy. I never once pulled back from love because I knew God loved me.

God revealed his presence even when I did not enter the gates of his sanctuary. God sanctified his calling on my life before the foundation of the world. He left me to explore my free will for twenty-six years. Then he said, "Enough." With his hooks, he pulled me in for his purposes, his plans, and my eternal benefit. I now praise him in all circumstances. God honors free will, but makes one willing to come to him.

God's Love and Protection

I finally left the relationship. But loneliness set in, and I reconciled with my husband under the condition that the physical and verbal abuse cease. Although he honored that request, I lowered my standards. At this point, my husband kept pushing for sharing partners (swinging). This discussion continued until I rationalized that, if he did what he wanted, there was no reason why I could not have fun. I did not realize that this type of fun is not of God. Lust lasts for a moment, but it eventually yields despair. This only brought the marriage relationship further away from the plans of God. The truth remains that one violates the body and self in this type of lifestyle. God's grace and mercy protected me from disease, as this lifestyle occurred before the era of AIDS. He saved me for my calling and my present husband, who truly loves me. A gamble happens when one has intimacy with over three hundred people. It only takes one mistake to destroy a life, and one can take on the spirit of all other sexual partners. Genesis 2:24 says, "Therefore shall a man leave his father and his mother, and shall cleave unto his wife: and they shall be one flesh." This truth means sexual intimacy is only for marriage, and only those two shall be one flesh.

God's Way in the Marriage Covenant

I am sharing this story to prevent others from the same anguish. God created man and woman for marriage. Marriage, God's divine way of intimacy, protects the individual in monogamy. In marriage, the husband becomes head of the wife to place her under the umbrella of God's protection. Many view submissiveness as a yoke and lack of freedom. But it remains the opposite. Submission exists for one's protection unless the husband asks the wife to alter from God's Word. A husband who loves his wife as Christ loves the church refrains from straying from God's ways. Otherwise, God deals with him to correct his ways and makes him willing to go. A wife's attempt to change her husband by nagging and yelling remains ineffective. I searched for love that I could have found all along from the Heavenly Father. God wants a praying wife who will come before him and pray for her husband. God revealed the preciousness of a marriage. No one can take away the intimacy with God.

A New Life

One morning after working the night shift, I returned home to find my husband and a portion of the furniture gone. I encountered the joys and heartbreaks of being alone. Our home was sold, and the proceeds were split as another dream vanished. My husband left after seven years of marriage and immediately married another woman. Even though I went through many difficulties, loneliness remained during this time. After the divorce, I attended school for my RN degree. I succeeded and completed my associate's degree while working full time. God's presence arose as I traveled back and forth from Lancaster to Harrisburg.

God's Continued Protection

I had to keep proving to others and myself, so I attended and graduated from Millersville University for my bachelor of science degree in nursing. Even in the midst of all this determination and stubbornness, God protected me. While driving home one morning after working a night shift, I fell asleep while driving. I heard a gentleman on the CB yelling, "Either that lady is drunk or asleep!" I abruptly woke up. This prevented me from being in an accident. God gave me this revelation and reminder, "Remember the time a man jumped out of his truck and held your car from going into the ditch. Afterwards, when you looked back, the truck was nowhere to be found. Truly, I sent an angel to prevent you from being hurt."

I continued to view success in terms of education as I enrolled in a master's program for nursing at the University of Arizona. However, I did not complete the degree. Exhaustion settled in as I scheduled eighty hours a week for work and school. In fact, my blood pressure elevated to 210/120. My blood pressure had always been normal prior to this incident. I leaned on my own understanding with this type of schedule. In addition, during this stressful time, God wanted me to slow down and smell the roses.

God's Love in the Midst of Wrong Choices

Six years after the divorce, I agreed to a second marriage to a handsome Native American man. We quickly drove to the courthouse for the marriage license before it closed. Then I phoned a minister who had placed a newspaper ad to perform the wedding ceremony. When he arrived, he was very short of breath. Relief came as he made it through the ceremony. Again, it was another marriage unequally yoked. God continued to love me despite wrong choices. God revealed years later, "Your heart remains part of the native community, both through Cherokee heritage and marriage."

Afterwards, my husband returned to Pennsylvania. Within a few months, I moved to South Carolina to complete the master's in nursing program at the University of South Carolina. With unhealthy eating habits and stress, my weight skyrocketed to one hundred and eighty pounds then rapidly dropped to one hundred and ten pounds through improved eating habits and a happier environment, thus creating a healthier frame on my petite body. During this time, I accepted an assistant director of nursing position for a two-hundred-and-fifty-bed facility. I flourished using God's gift of leadership.

With all the education and success in the workplace, I neglected the most important aspect of life: my husband. After graduation, I returned to Pennsylvania with my husband and accepted a position as a director of nursing in a small nursing facility. I remained content for a year. Then I began to feel I lacked my full professional potential. I returned to a career with the previous nursing home chain as a director of nursing in North Carolina and then Georgia.

My previous supervisor later asked me to accept a position as vice president of nursing for twelve facilities. I arrived at the brink of success, according to my understanding. During this time, I proceeded to complete a master's in business administration program (MBA) at Kennesaw University. Even with all this knowledge and drive, I again failed to prioritize my marriage.

During this time, my second husband started having a fancy for another woman. I asked him to stop, but his unwillingness prevailed. My anger came to the forefront. Instead of forgiving him, I ran. Although I continued to visit about every two months, this could not reestablish trust or reaffirm love. Even though God created this time to slow me down and return to my husband, I did not see it this way. Determined, I continued on the path to success that the world had defined. I did not receive love from my husband, so I turned to a woman while searching for love. Even in the midst of ungodly choices, God allows us to have our own will. Yet he waited patiently for my return as I grew farther away.

One day, my supervisor was speaking with me, and I said, "I wish I had a relationship with a woman." This opened the door for the evil one, and he took advantage. In the meantime, I visited my husband, who continued to refuse to refrain from seeing the other woman, so I continued on the path of destruction. The devastating words spoken would lead my life farther away from God. I looked at the situation through my own eyes, and the evil one entered my thoughts. How could I think I would find true love in this manner? God's love remains the only true love.

Within two weeks, a friend introduced me to a woman. The first time we met, she wanted to commit. The Holy Spirit maintained a presence by creating uneasiness in my spirit for several months. I did not listen, and it gradually became easier to say yes to a commitment ceremony. Two weeks before the ceremony, I divorced for the second time. During the ceremony, I literally cried so hard that I fell to the ground. God revealed, "The Holy Spirit grieved because you made a commitment to the evil one and caused an abomination in the sight of God. You did not realize how I wanted you back. As you drove to the ceremony, two deer crossed your path. This indicated I remained in the midst of everything."

Things worked well in the relationship. I had a great job and started classes for my MBA. After I completed the MBA, I proceeded to use my expertise by incorporating and building an assisted living center for seniors, which opened in 1997. This business created the pinnacle of my career as CEO of my own company.

God's Continual Presence

God had other things in mind to bring me to himself and to humble me. The evil one portrayed himself as light, making everything appear good, which ended in havoc and confusion. That's when God said, "Enough! You remain mine. Come back to me because I have the victory." My life ended up so far from Jesus. I never dreamed of experiencing abuse, swinging, or being involved in a lesbian relationship. I was not this precious little girl that my parents had brought up in the church. This devastation occurred when I believed lies from the evil one. Although I had accepted Jesus as Lord and

Savior, I failed to have a personal relationship with him. You may not have experienced these exact circumstances, but, whatever your circumstances, I challenge you to look at a walk with Jesus. Consider a relationship with Jesus now. Without him, one is separated from God, spending eternity without hope. The only way to God comes through accepting his son Jesus, who died for our sins. Accept him now as you read, and allow Jesus into your heart and life so you can spend eternity in heaven.

Masks Don't Work

In actuality, I lived two lives because others did not know all the deeds of the prodigal daughter. They only knew the "nice" Cynthia. Nice and masks do not work. They only hide things for a season. Then you have nowhere to turn except to God. Otherwise, one proceeds deeper into the wiles of the evil one, ending in destruction. The good news rings out when one repents and asks forgiveness of the Lord. He will cleanse white as snow and cover you with his precious blood, no matter what you have done. The slate clears when one repents. This does not mean that one evades correction but the correction yields the peaceable fruit of righteousness. God maintains his hand in every circumstance.

Now no chastening for the present seemeth to be joyous, but grievous: nevertheless afterward it yieldeth the peaceable fruit of righteousness unto them which are exercised thereby.

Heb 12:11

CHAPTER THREE
A BRAND PLUCKED OUT
OF THE FIRE

This chapter speaks to those who think the turmoil will never end. God has everyone in his loving arms. God's presence increases at the most crucial moment of one's life. I felt angry and without peace as I journeyed through all the difficulties. But the Lord later revealed to me how he rescued me from destruction and kept me from physical death, as in Ps 118:18, "The LORD hath chastened me sore: but hath not given me over unto death." At times during the trials, I felt like Job, as he expressed himself in Job 19:9–10, "He hath stripped me of my glory, and taken the crown from my head. He hath destroyed me on every side, and I am gone: and mine hope hath he removed like a tree."

God's Love through Chastening

On August 5, 1999, as I completed my daily routine at the assisted living center, to my surprise, the doors flew open with several police officers. They presented me with a search warrant. They kept me busy finding files. One moment, I went to the kitchen with thoughts of fleeing this nightmare. A policeman followed, so I remained calm. After several hours, they arrested me. God arranged this arrest to bring me back unto him. A few months earlier, I had refused to give back the initial deposit to a resident's family. I was determined to keep the deposit for damages incurred. The daughter stated she knew the district attorney and would have my arrest broadcast in the local newspaper. That's exactly what happened. There I sat in the holding cell, in my suit and heels, feeling numb and devastated. Years later, as I read Lam 3:13, "He hath caused the arrows of his quiver to enter into my reins," I realized that's exactly what I experienced.

A former supervisor posted bail. He placed his home as collateral. Within six hours, they released me. God's mercy prevailed as I was not processed nor did I spend time in jail. I shook that night, and I could barely sleep. God showed me that I had nothing to fear, as I later claimed the verse in 2 Tim 1:7, "For God hath not given us the spirit of fear; but of power, and of love, and of a sound mind." I humbled myself and returned to work as usual. The actual court date did not occur until a year and a half later. In the meantime, I managed the facility, addressing the concerns of the employees and family members.

Six months later, the state arrived and requested I cease as the administrator, or they would close the facility. Now this truly devastated my reputation. A few days prior, I had interviewed a candidate for the assistant administrator position, so I phoned her, and she took the position. God arranged for the management of the facility while taking away my control. Isaiah 54:8 is one Scripture I keep close to my heart to reveal God's mercy: "In a little wrath I hid my face from thee for a moment; but with everlasting kindness will I have mercy on thee, saith the Lord thy redeemer."

I realized God's scourging came from my long-term rebellion. This scourging ran deep into my heart. It happened to be more than the discipline of God stepping in to lift me from my own destructive and unfruitful pursuits. It appeared more than God getting my attention or more than a rebuke or verbal warning. I made poor choices, and God wanted to spare me further pain. It also appeared more than chastening, where one feels emotional anxiety, frustration, and distress. I had ongoing disobedience in my life, keeping me from God's best. In fact, the scourging I experienced could be considered as excruciating pain. God shouted, took my long-term disobedience seriously, and acted accordingly. My scourging came after twenty-six years of lust and ungodly relationships.

The court date finally arrived, which resulted in a five-year probation that required a monthly visit to the probation officer. I grew more upset each month, questioning and feeling that I did not deserve these circumstances. I would often read my Bible while I waited, which gave me peace. I realized how God comforted me during this time with Psalms and Proverbs.

I attended seminars out of state once or twice a month, requiring written permission each time. God, in his mercy, provided less restriction by the granting of monthly permissions. This highly unusual protocol remained until the end of my probation. I attended a seminar in Florida when the regulations changed. They had required I register with the nearest police station when I was out of state. Terror enveloped me. A blessing came when one of the women from the seminar had empathy to accompany me. She experienced the same thing in her life so she understood. In the midst of one trial after another, God remained present. He chastises his sons and daughters out of love so they will return to him. The ability to attend the seminars lessened the restrictions in work and other areas. God knows what each person can handle. A jail term would have caused deep anger and bitterness instead of coming closer to God. In 2003, I truly forgave the resident's daughter, employees, police, and entire community. But the most important part entailed forgiving myself for my lack of integrity and participation in an ungodly lifestyle.

Most importantly, after three years, I completed the probation. My criminal record was wiped clean because it was considered a first-time offense. That's what Jesus does for each person. He takes away the record of our disobedience and washes the slate clean. I did not realize the extent of my separation from God until he said:

> Enough, young lady! You did quite enough on your own, and I had you apprehended. This chastisement and brokenness brought you back to me. I shattered your identity so you would return. Your heart became hardened because you did not want men to hurt you anymore. My Holy Spirit grieved when you turned to a lesbian relationship. I removed all pride and left you humble. I took

you by the hook, as this remained the only way to bring you back. You went through pain, but it yielded the peaceable fruit of righteousness. It also turned out to be an avenue for you to share the good news about my purpose on Earth. You looked for love and finally found it in me, not in your husband, business, or more schooling. You forgave others, but harassing thoughts continued until you forgave yourself.

Shame disappeared when God enlightened and delivered me from destruction. Truth set me free. God took me through a preparation time, a time of separation and dealing with my outward man. The process of breaking the outward man occurs gradually; otherwise, the flesh would fast-forward before he revealed the entire truth. Only then can God instill the revelations into the heart. I also heard God's still-small voice say, "Know that I am in everything. When you speak, I want them to see me rather than Cynthia. I chastise those I love. Otherwise, going through life without difficulties, one settles for less. At best, success. At worst, destruction."

Watchman Nee's book, *Release of the Spirit*, gave insight into accepting my circumstances through these words:

God always shows us how hateful and polluted we

are, and our immediate response is: Alas! What a wretch I am, so unclean, so despicable! For God to reveal our true self is to fall down as dead. Once a proud person has been truly enlightened, he cannot so much as make an attempt to be proud anymore. The effect of enlightenment will have its mark upon him all his days. On the other hand, this time of enlightenment is also the time for believing, not for asking, but for bowing low. God follows the same principle in saving us as He does in working with us afterwards. When the radiancy of the gospel shines upon us, we do not pray: Lord, I beseech Thee to be my Savior. To pray this, even for days, would bring no assurance of salvation. We simply say: Lord I receive Thee to be my Savior. Instantly salvation happens! In like manner, in God's subsequent working, as soon as light comes upon us we should immediately prostrate ourselves under His light and tell the Lord: Lord, I accept Thy sentence I agree with Thy judgment. This will prepare us for more light.[8]

---

8 Watchman Nee, *Release of the Spirit* (Cloverdale, Indiana: Sure Foundation, 1965), 79.

God's Purpose Revealed

This process of accepting my situation took five years. God revealed to me:

> I had no other way to bring you back to the fold except to literally shake your spirit. You have free will so I made you willing to come. This was one of the most transforming days of your life. The devastation occurred so you would share my message with man. I started the process of having you willing to come. You experienced disbelief, shock, and later embarrassment, but I kept you from that travesty of spending time in jail. I walked beside you each time you went to the probation office. You read my Word as you waited with nowhere else to turn. I needed you in this place of humbleness. I took every part of your being apart. Literally, no self remained. Shame caused the inability to speak about your situation for two years. Anger arose as they searched your assisted living facility because you considered this a sacred place for the residents. Remember I give everything, including the assisted living. You heard the angry words of the resident's daughter exclaim, and you denied the possibility of her words. The wrath of man roars like a lion. Afterwards, you

remembered the daughter spoke of being abused.
You realized her hurt and forgave her. The hurts
that need healing cause hurt to others. You had
a difficult time forgiving yourself. As the process
and journey deepened, you forgave yourself. This
is when true healing began. You forgave all the
others who hurt you and gave up being right.
Forgiving self and giving up being right resulted in
learning two important lessons. This chastisement
included the integrity issue, the deposit issue,
and the years you spent in disobedience. Once
your heart attitude changed, the peaceable fruit
of righteousness flowed forth. The facility was the
baby you birthed. With your identity destroyed,
your pride took a nosedive, and I placed you in a
humble condition in total devastation without a
job as your life dream vanished. You interviewed
the administrator, thinking that lack of funds
could not warrant hiring her. My plans remain
higher. I already provided the administrator
before you needed one. When she accepted the
position, you left and never returned. You loved
the residents too much to allow the closing of
the facility. I provided a place for these residents
to live. These dreams I planted in your heart,
even though you built without asking. Your

calling as a prophetess did not include continued management of the facility. My plans of you reaching millions through the healing ministry far outweighed your goal of building thirty facilities. As you searched for a job, you felt the nightmare would never end. After the three years of probation, you again had no criminal background. Instead of joy, you continued to hurt. Fear destroyed your personhood. You always remained free in all the midst of your trials. You traveled to seminars in different states. No other person on probation traveled this extensively. My design created a space so you would feel less restricted. Because you viewed that time as terror, fear overrode your faith. The evil one wanted you back. I would not allow that because I purposed you for a high calling since the foundation of the world. Those failures, a stepping-stone for my successes, brought you back to my throne room. In addition, the battles you experienced with the community and employees as part of your chastisement eventually increased your faith. The decisions you make as your ministry unfolds will result in my victory.

Divine Appointment

During this time, my partner suffered a major seizure. The doctors diagnosed her with an arterial venous malformation (AVM), a tangle of abnormal and poorly formed blood vessels, both arteries and veins. Two months after the seizure, the doctors scheduled surgery; otherwise, a massive brain bleed could occur. A week prior to her surgery, while attending a seminar, I encountered a divine appointment. I sat beside a chaplain who worked at the same hospital where the doctor scheduled my partner's surgery. She agreed to see her at the hospital. We did not attend church at the time so this visit comforted her. The brain surgery lasted fourteen hours. During the surgery, I went to the chapel and cried out to God. Neither one of us fully comprehended the full extent of the involvement of the rehabilitation process. Instead of taking six weeks for recovery, as the doctors stated, she endured two years of rehabilitation. We both had a difficult time. Accustomed to caring for others, this circumstance remained very different because this care took twenty-four hours a day without relief.

God's Goodness in the Midst of Poor Choices

During my morning devotions one day, the Lord showed me this revelation:

I gave you the grace to care for her for a year and

a half. It would not have been possible to care for her if you worked. She did not have anyone else to care for her during this long process of rehabilitation. This burden you found too difficult to bear yourself, so I provided the invitation to church. This is what brought you back to me. This first step of accepting the invitation caused you to come back into the fold. With no one around, you cried for your deceased mother. Your partner could not help. You searched for help, but I remained with you through this entire journey. You took the next step and finally released the relationship. Looking back, you saw how I had you in my loving arms. I had to deal with her issues of disobedience and yours.

These difficult times caused me to return to God. The scourging actually lasted a short time compared to the destiny and calling upon my life. The Lord spoke to me:

I had to woo my prodigal daughter back. I accepted you as I turned your scarlet robe into white and your pride into humbleness. Your disobedience and arrogance appeared very similar to Saul's downfall. However, in my mercy and grace, I refined the dirt into gold.

I discerned and chose to accept the chastisement, not

only to return to God, but to share what God accomplished in me through the return to his loving arms. I would not be able to understand what anyone went through unless I had a similar experience. Watchman Nee's book, *Release of the Spirit*, verbalized exactly what the Lord revealed:

> All our circumstances are ordered by God. Nothing is accidental. God's ordering is according to His knowledge of our needs, and with a view to the shattering of the outward man. Knowing that a certain external thing will thus affect us, He arranges for us to encounter it once, twice, and perhaps even more. Do you not realize that all the events of your life for the past five or ten years were ordered by God for your education? If you murmured and complained, you grievously failed to recognize His hand. If you thought you were unfortunate, you were in ignorance of the discipline of the Holy Spirit. Remember that whatever happens to us is measured by the hand of God for our supreme good.[9]

The final loss of the facility through foreclosure and bankruptcy of personal and business assets caused the final blow to my identity. Consequently, the stress initiated a six-week battle with pneumonia. I could not

---

9 Watchman Nee, *Release of the Spirit* (Cloverdale, Indiana: Sure Foundation, 1965), 59.

understand how things could get this low. I realized what really happened when I read *Release of the Spirit*:

> Again and again God arranges our circumstances
> to break us in our strong point. You may be
> stricken once, twice, but still the third blow must
> come. God will not let you go. He will not stay
> His hand until He has broken that prominent
> feature in you.[10]

This final circumstance released my strong feature of pride. Humbled and without control, God placed me where he wanted me. When one repents, God forgives and cleanses. The transformation may happen immediately, or it may be a process. Regardless, God always welcomes one back into the fold, no matter what the journey may entail.

---

10 Watchman Nee, *Release of the Spirit* (Cloverdale, Indiana: Sure Foundation, 1965), 77.

But he knoweth the way that I take: when he hath tried me, I shall come forth as gold.

Job 23:10

Chapter Four
Back to the Fold

The Invitation

The return to the fold happened when a friend invited my partner and me to church, and we accepted the invitation. This milestone returned me to God's turf. I had not been in a church setting for twenty-six years. The Holy Spirit worked vigorously in my heart. It wasn't the church but the rededication to Jesus Christ and God that transformed my life. This allowed an open heart for the Holy Spirit to work. More transformation, rededication, cleansing, and repentance occurred after my baptism.

Disobedience Cleansed

Prior to the baptism by immersion, my partner gave me a Bible and wrote the following blessing found in Numbers

6:24–26, "The LORD bless thee, and keep thee: The LORD make his face shine upon thee, and be gracious unto thee: the LORD lift up his countenance upon thee, and give thee peace."

The Lord revealed to me that, when my partner wrote the Scripture, this released me from the commitment. Then the Holy Spirit could work. God deleted all those years of disobedience from my record after my baptism. The pastor requested I be baptized when I decided to join the church but I lacked the understanding of the full significance of the baptism. Similar to the baptism unto Moses, I walked out of Egypt into the promised land. With all the heartbreak caused by disobedience cleansed, I returned pure to the Father. I later comprehended the importance of baptism by immersion as an important aspect of a transformed life. With everything washed away, I no longer continued in my old ways. Convicted of my disobedience, God wiped away the past and brought me out of the fire, pure as gold. This process took time. If the cocoon is opened before its time, one will not fly as a butterfly. Instead, one will wither and die.

This process took five years because of the distraction of past experiences. A spiritual battle ensued, and the evil one did not want to release me. Finally, in God's perfect timing, I surrendered everything to God. Then God gave me my perfect husband. The Holy Spirit wooed me, love surrounded me, and his arms enveloped me. I once again returned to holy ground. This time, I would have a relationship with Jesus and know him personally, not in a formal way. My Abba Father wiped away all the twenty-six years of disobedience. He welcomed me back like the prodigal daughter. He would not allow my destruction because of his mercy and grace. He knew what would cause me to have a deep relationship with him and forsake my own will.

The sermons and the ladies Bible study continued to water me. This rebuilt the foundation I needed to return to the fold. God healed my body, my soul, and my spirit. One very meaningful Scripture is 2 Chr 7:14, "If my people, which are called by my name, shall humble themselves, and pray, and seek my face, and turn from their wicked ways; then will I hear from Heaven, and will forgive their sin, and will heal their land."

I grew in the Lord as the Holy Spirit touched me during the teachings from the pastor and ladies ministry. At this time, I lacked friends to guide me closer to God. He designed things this way so I would follow in his ways and not the ways of man. The Holy Spirit moved as I formed a relationship with Jesus. Although the evil one kept presenting many temptations, various philosophies, and lusts, God had the victory and would not allow me to stray again.

I saw his grace and mercy in my life. God took away the shame. I replaced that shame with a knowing that all of my wayward circumstances would help others over the rough spots by sharing his glory and my deliverance with millions. God taught me to savor the moments of each day by spending time with him. He taught me to praise in difficult times in spite of not really understanding. In the wilderness, where I learned the most, I heard his voice to discern his direction for my life. One insight the Lord revealed included, "Listen when someone is upset. Ask yourself, 'Is this person hurting, or does it come from your disobedience?'"

The Holy Spirit continued to work in my heart. During my participation in a Beth Moore study, it became clear that I wore a veil that had to be shed because Christ shed his blood for me. It was a long veil of abuse, arrest, bankruptcy, foreclosure, and divorce. It was a veil of feeling unwanted and being a victim. It was a veil of helplessness, shame, withholding, and ungodly relationships. Then I realized, as God's child, his blood cleansed all circumstances.

Now I can go hand in hand with the Lord. After my rebellion, I looked back and saw a single set of footprints as God carried me through my testing, chastisement, and trials. God wanted me unto himself, but he would not go against my will. God is the great alchemist turning dirt into gold, as in Job 23:10, "When he hath tried me, I shall come forth as gold." Two other Scriptures that reflected my life include:

- "For as the heavens are higher than the earth, so are my ways higher than your ways, and my thoughts than your thoughts" (Isa 55:9).

- "But I would ye should understand, brethren, that the things which happened unto me have fallen out rather unto the furtherance of the gospel" (Phil 1:12).

God shared the following,

Your body is a temple, and I cleansed it. But
this followed repentance. I cleansed your body
white as snow, no longer defiled, for my will.
I swept all the rooms clean. I turned the ashes
into beauty. Nourish your temple with healthy
food and exercise. The keys to the temple include
diligence, prayer, fasting, purity, and integrity.
With obedience, I can then align your body for
wholeness. You went without a song for twenty-
six years prior to coming back to me. When I take

disobedience off the record, I wash the slate clean.
I want you to share my glory and your deliverance
with the world.

Rededication

Then my partner talked about suicide one day. Her
mother had committed suicide when she was eighteen,
so I did not take those words lightly. She complied with
admission to the hospital. Part of the rededication to
Jesus included sharing with the pastor. The Holy Spirit
rose up inside me. As soon as the hospital completed the
admission, I drove to the church and shared my story.
There remained no question now about leaving the
relationship. He counseled me, and I denounced the past
and repented. God tells us that our body is a temple. Now
that I knew God's ways, leaving this ungodly relationship
left no regrets or feelings of loss.

Even after the rededication of my life to Jesus,
difficulties continued because of the lack of knowledge
of the importance of putting on the armor every day.
New to the relationship with Jesus, I had an open
heart for his Word and the ways of his divine plan as
the Holy Spirit continued to woo me. Even though I
accepted Jesus as Savior, I did not realize the depth of this
relationship. During those five years, the church shared

the truth through the Word, and I began to know God intimately.

This transformation completely changed the relationship that I surmised as love. I previously accepted this relationship with a woman as being okay because I continued to feel the hurt from the two previous marriages. In God's eyes, this disobedience remained unacceptable, so he broke the covenant from the commitment ceremony and continued to show his hand.

Open Doors

As I made plans to leave this relationship, a family opened their home. I thought the stay would be temporary, perhaps for a month. But this part of the journey lasted one year. That year marked a divine keeping from God. This opportunity opened up because I accepted God's will. That family will be blessed because they gave me free room and board because I could not work at this point. I did occasionally care for their twin boys. God gave them the heart to do this. God knows every detail of our lives. Psalm 68:6, "God setteth the solitary in families," came to life during that year. As the year ended, I knew things had to change. The time came to find another place to live. The family later accepted Jesus as their Savior because of the seeds of faith I had planted.

God provided a job with a nursing agency and the

opportunity to move. I received a phone call from a friend looking for a roommate. I agreed. A year later, God placed in my heart the desire to purchase my own home. During this time, God brought me through the heartbreak of the foreclosure of the facility. I also experienced bankruptcy for everything, including the corporate issues. The miracle happened when I purchased a new home six months after bankruptcy. The blessing of my beautiful three-bedroom home, two minutes from the church, came to fruition as I kept in obedience to the Lord.

God provided for a mission trip to Thailand. I had faith and purchased the airplane ticket four months before I could travel to another country. I believed God would complete his plan. The Holy Spirit strengthened me as I continued in God's will. Denial did not exist even though I had not completed probation. God had me willing to lose the money I spent for the ticket even if I could not go. I continued to appropriate faith, knowing God had everything under control. One month after the purchase of the ticket, the pardon arrived, leaving me without a criminal background so I could take the journey to Thailand. God opens doors when one's faith arises. I traveled to speak with high school students who came to know Jesus as a result of my testimony. During this time,

I assisted a missionary teaching English to these students who appeared so eager to speak the English language.

During the mission trip, I learned and grew in God's purposes. God can change circumstances in a moment. This is why I stay on his path. He gives the faith and grace to come through all circumstances and to give back to others.

Prayer of Relinquishment

One night, I prayed the prayer of relinquishment and gave my will to God, saying, "Lord, I want to be married because I have the passion that burns. However, your will be done. If you want me to be single, I will follow you." The Lord later revealed:

> The day you were prone and relinquished
> everything to me, I made a covenant and returned
> your glory. I became your husband, and I gave
> you an earthly husband. Always remember me as
> your first love. Then the abundant blessings flow.
> Night shift took a toll on your body. Now I have
> renewed, refreshed, cleansed, and healed you.
> The years of stress have lifted off as you remained
> under my protection.

Two months after that prayer, I logged on to an

Internet dating site and e-mailed this gentleman in Canada. We corresponded by e-mail and phone. We eventually decided to meet, and I flew to Canada to meet him. After a walk in the park during this brief visit, he asked me to marry him. Excited, I immediately said yes. I shared my testimony in the first e-mail. I wanted this third marriage to be different by being God-centered. In the meantime, George himself had an encounter with the Lord. In his profile from the Internet dating site, he stated that any eligible woman could only be single or widow, not a divorcée. Through a series of e-mails, the Lord spoke to him clearly from Acts 10:15, "What God has cleansed that call not thou common." Now George had been brought up in the truth of the Word, and a divorcée never entered the picture. Then God worked in his heart in such a soft way that, in George's own words, "Without any debate or guilt, I accepted what the Lord said to Peter in Acts 10:15 that I felt totally at ease asking Cynthia to marry me upon her visit to Canada."

I immediately recognized George as the godly man I prayed for. He spoke about little else except Jesus. I did not know that what unfolded would turn out to be more precious than I could imagine. This has me praise God for every situation. God took every tear, every trial, and every moment of loneliness. I returned to the fold, and he opened up the heavens with his wonderful mercy and grace. Two verses that God shared because I waited and acknowledged his will for my life are included:

- "Rest in the LORD, and wait patiently for him" (Ps 37:7).

- "In all thy ways acknowledge him, and he shall direct thy paths" (Prv 3:6).

On April 16, 2005, the physical manifestation of this marriage happened, arranged by God from the foundation of the world. The Lord said to me:

> You knew you had something big to give to the
> world. I answered you with the highest calling
> of reconciling my people and a healing ministry.
> I took away a physical job and redirected you to
> the spiritual realm with a calling that is my will.
> I wanted your ministry incorporated with your
> husband. I designed for the two of you to use your
> gifts, experiences, and weaknesses to demonstrate
> to the world what I can do.

God fulfilled that desire I had as a child for a wonderful marriage and children and fulfilled his promise to bring forth my destiny. I now know the truth of II Pet 3:9, "The Lord is not slack concerning his promise, as some men count slackness; but is longsuffering to us-ward, not willing that any should perish, but that all should come to repentance."

During this time of coming back to the fold, God dealt with me on many issues. It became a time of brokenness, transparency, and giving everything to God.

Although the fig tree shall not blossom, neither shall fruit be in the vines; the labour of the olive shall fail, and the fields shall yield no meat; the flock shall be cut off from the fold, and there shall be no herd in the stalls: Yet I will rejoice in the LORD, I will joy in the God of my salvation. The LORD is my strength, and he will make my feet like hinds' feet, and he will make me to walk upon mine high places.

Hab 3:17–19

CHAPTER FIVE
BROKENNESS

Release of Indifference and Pride

Brokenness is the process of getting to the cross and coming to God. He placed me in the heat of the fire of brokenness and released my pride. God took my relationship, business, home, car, identity, and reputation. God said:

> You became too big for your britches. I had to get you off your pedestal. You thought your strength came from all your degrees and business. I revealed myself through these trials. In this brokenness, I shed the veil from your eyes. The brokenness brought renewal and transformation to your life by renewing of your mind and

acknowledging your disobedience. In this process, you gave your life to me. The Holy Spirit showed you the wrong choices and how I loved you in the midst of those ungodly choices. Seeing the trials as an experience of chastening brought you to humbleness, which occurred after you repented, asked forgiveness, and acknowledged the indifference, disobedience, and pride.

When I got out of the way, God could work. Listen to God's heartstrings, not feelings. It is important to learn the lessons from the trials. I praise God for my circumstances that brought me closer to him. Interruptions of life are opportunities to learn lessons. I now refrain from bitterness toward these interruptions. I grew in God's mercy, grace, and glory during these experiences. I am reminded that all gold has passed through the fire, every jewel has gone through pressure, and every pearl has been subjected to suffering.

Integrity with Holiness and Purity

Another aspect that God broke included the issue of integrity. God placed me on holy ground, and I could no longer walk in the ways of impurity. I realized that small things eventually add up to a mound of dirt that one cannot easily vacuum away. God's love touched me, so how could I not walk in his ways? God convicted me of all areas of disobedience to his Word that did not align with his promises. The area most prevalent remained my passion. God did not take away the passion, but redirected it for his timing in my marriage to George. I heard God say:

> Dance with me and allow my timing to surround
> all you do. My promises are yea and amen. Be
> joyous in the waiting, my child, for the time
> is near where I bless you beyond what you can
> comprehend. I made you reflector of light to
> the world. Keep in my guidance. A shut door
> indicates my move, as does an open door. I kissed
> you with my Father's power. With tenderness, I
> shielded you from the past. I sanctified you, so
> rest in my loving arms that will not fail. I became
> your husband. Never forget I am your first love.
> You remain at total peace as you released the past.
> My grace is perfect, and I want you to share this
> with the world.

God's Healing of Anger

The issue of anger of past hurts had to be broken. The circumstances that happened to me caused resentments at having to prove myself. The anger also fired up when things did not go my way. This anger was bottled up inside, withholding the anger until it would occasionally explode with a real upset. This affected the liver, the seat of anger, causing elevated liver enzymes. In his graciousness and mercy, God slowly dissipated my anger. Then my health returned through the healing of Jesus, exercise, and an herb called milk thistle. God spoke:

> Do not worry about what others will think or say because you will speak my words. I want no withholding. You must tell all. Keep me first. I give you the desires of your heart, even when it appears differently than you think. Continue to submit to my will, walk in forgiveness, and remain in integrity. Ride my waves and experience the blessings. I give you supernatural protection.

Good Thoughts Equal Good Health

God revealed to me that individuals cram God into less than 10 percent of the brain in the natural realm. God wants everyone in his image utilizing 90 percent of their brain in the spiritual realm. When you deal with the emotions without allowing them to fester inside, then the real person appears because the dross is gone. When the brain and heart line up with God's promises, one makes good decisions. This alignment occurs as one brings all thoughts to the Lord's table of acceptance or rejection, accepting truth and allowing the Holy Spirit's presence. This entails acknowledging all lies. When one takes thoughts captive, it becomes easier to form the good thoughts. Brain scans visualize bad thoughts as actual darkened thorns; good thoughts appear as trees and beautiful flowers.

Forgiveness and Cleansing

I knew I had to forgive everyone, including myself. Once I forgave, a peace came into my heart. I realized I had the opportunity, privilege, and responsibility to teach others about forgiveness. I could not allow my hurts to immobilize me, so I decided to turn those hurts into a valuable resource to encourage and equip others to forgive. Whether one uses the hurts in a negative or positive way depends on if one forgives others and oneself.

When I left the lesbian relationship, God immediately took away those feelings. Breaking free can be that easy as God enters the heart. God loves unconditionally, but he will not approve a lifestyle of disobedience. In a conversation regarding this type of lifestyle, ask how the past may have turned one to this type of lifestyle. Pray for God to place the right people in one's path and soften the heart to see the truth about the path chosen. Do not condone the sin, but love the person. So do not judge. Rather, determine not to put an obstacle in a brother's way. The Bible remains clear about homosexuality, even though it is widely accepted. 1 Corinthians 6:9–10 states,

"Know ye not that the unrighteous shall not inherit the kingdom of God? Be not deceived: neither fornicators, nor idolaters, nor adulterers, nor effeminate, nor abusers of themselves with mankind, nor thieves, nor covetous, nor drunkards, nor revilers, nor extortioners, shall inherit the kingdom of God."

Know that God forgives and wants as many as possible to receive eternal life. This happens with repentance. The evil one likes to muddy the waters with lies and deceit. Jesus is the only one to fill the void of trying to capture love outside of marriage.

Intimacy in Marriage

God created sex as a powerful gift within marriage. He sets parameters for healthy sexual intimacy as a sacred bond between a husband and a wife. This protects and allows one to enjoy that intimacy to the fullest. God gave sex as a wedding gift to married couples. Christians and non-Christians bound and mastered by their sexual desires become deadened to hearing God's voice. Satan tempts married couples into adultery and even lack of intimacy. This grieves the Father, but he forgives everything when one comes to him and repents. Romans 10:11 has comforted me, "Whosoever believeth on him shall not be ashamed."

God's Love Brought Me Back to His Loving Arms

The Lord spoke:

> You could no longer continue with the destructive
> path. This included being out of integrity,
> rebelling, and seeking your own pleasures without
> a care what it did to others or your temple. I
> love my children. I could not allow this path to
> continue, but I could not go against your will,
> so I created situations I knew would cause you
> to return to me. I grieved all those years that I
> could not be close to you, but I remained with
> you during the trials and tribulations. I love you.
> That is why I could not allow disobedience to
> continue. I know those times were full of pain and
> heartbreak. With your whole identity destroyed,
> you had to die to self as you lost everything.
> I brought you to the last straw. As you placed
> Cynthia first, you could not see or hear me. You
> cried many tears for I placed you in a position
> where you had no one to rely on except me. Those
> tears remain in a bottle because the tears faded as
> your eyes opened to my ways. Going through the
> trauma, I strengthened you with my strength. I
> carried you with my grace and mercy and kissed

each tear that fell. I know the beginning and the end of your life. I know the great calling I designed for you, even through those tears where you said, "I cannot take it anymore." It took time, but you saw my glory, grace, and mercy. Now you would not trade those moments of trials for anything because now there remains a bonded relationship that cannot be broken. Through the brokenness, you saw my love. This love is greater than any human love. For everyone who is searching and has come to his or her wit's end, I am the answer. Yes, you do not welcome pain. But the peace that passes all understanding came forth as you came out of the fire and followed my ways. In brokenness, one realizes that the worldly things appear small compared to an eternal life.

Citizenship in Heaven

God chose to create me. The death of Jesus allowed me to be the King's child. In the kingdom, one obeys the king's words. The king appoints ambassadors, so I am an ambassador for Jesus. If someone hurts me, this becomes an international incident and God protects. God deals with them. In the kingdom, I have citizenship in heaven. The king owns the country, land, people, animals, and trees. Each individual authority over Earth comes from

Jesus because he remains King of kings and Lord of lords.

From Natural Gentleness to Spiritual Fruit

I wore a mask of niceness and did not want it uncovered or revealed because of all the shame. I wore the mask of niceness as long as everything went well. When God removed the mask, my life began to be real and transparent in his image. Now my life flourishes not on feelings but on the grace and direction of God. The Lord gradually dispersed this duplicity as I shared with trusted friends. The freedom opened, the fear subsided, and the shame faded away as the truth brought everything to light. When God broke the niceness, that natural gentleness became spiritual fruit as the Holy Spirit took control. I understood this when I read *Release of the Spirit* by Watchman Nee:

> First, all that is natural is independent of the spirit, while all that comes through the discipline of the Holy Spirit is under the spirit's control, moving only as the spirit moves. Natural gentleness can really become a hindrance to the spirit. One who is habitually gentle is gentle in himself, not in the Lord. Suppose the Lord wants him to stand up and utter some strong words. His natural gentleness will hinder him from following

the Lord. He would say instead, Ah, this I cannot do. I have never uttered such hard words. Let someone else do it. I simply cannot. You see how his natural gentleness is not under the spirit's control. Anything that is natural has its own will and is independent of the spirit. However, that gentleness which comes through brokenness can be used by the spirit, for it does not resist nor offer its own opinion. Second, a naturally gentle person is gentle only while you are going along with his will. If you force him to do what he does not like, he will change his attitude. In so called human virtues, the element of self denial is lacking. It is obvious the purpose of all them is to build up and establish our self life. Whenever that self is violated, the human virtues all disappear. The virtues which spring from discipline, on the other hand, are only possessed after our ugly self-life has been destroyed. Where God is breaking your self, there true virtue is seen. The more self is wounded, the brighter shines true gentleness. Natural gentleness and spiritual fruit, then, are basically different.[11]

---

11 Watchman Nee, *Release of the Spirit* (Cloverdale, Indiana: Sure Foundation, 1965), 93–94.

The King's Child

I feared rejection so I acted nice to receive love, focusing only on myself. I now share truth, and I am concerned for the welfare of others. I masked selfishness and insincerity with politeness and niceness until I realized I am the King's child. God transformed that fear of rejection, selfishness, and insincerity into eyes that see only his love.

Fine-tuning

It appeared my circumstances would never end during these five years of brokenness. Then, I heard God say:

I fine-tuned you through adversity and your brokenness. Now dance to the music of my words. When I move, follow the same direction for my desires become your desires. My Holy Spirit works in full power. Refrain from looking back because now my glory springs forth. Maybe the world refused to hear you, but I hear. My words and healing flow forth, causing others to believe.

I found out that God had to perfect me so I could learn the lessons and fully return to him. It says in Isa 30:18, "And therefore will the LORD wait, that he may be gracious unto you, and therefore will he be exalted, that he may have mercy upon you: for the LORD is a God of judgment: blessed are all they that wait for him."

Cleansed White as Snow

God cleansed me, as in Acts 10:28, "God hath shewed me that I should not call any man common or unclean," and Acts 10:15, "What God has cleansed, that call not thou common." This period of brokenness became a time where the lies had to be torn down about abuse, failed marriages, and ungodly relationships. Several of the lies that had to be torn down included:

- All men would hurt me, and I could do nothing.

- I could not say no.

- If people knew my previous disobedience, I'd be destroyed.

It took twenty-six years before I would share about the ungodly relationships and two years before I could even say the word "arrest." The tactics of the evil one to isolate and hide secrets creates a place of darkness. 1 John 1:9 says, "If we confess our sins, he is faithful and just to forgive us our sins, and to cleanse us from all unrighteousness." The bonds broke, and freedom occurred when I confessed my disobedience.

Dying to Self

I learned I must continually release my will to him and, in obedience and repentance, ask forgiveness. I could not truly understand this until I realized the need to die to self daily. This daily process of dying to self includes knowing Jesus died for our sins. We need to give everything to God daily. I did not understand this until I understood his ways that, in all the circumstances of life, God has his hand in everything.

Freedom

God took the shame and embarrassment and replaced it with freedom. I no longer had to be a victim. God sent Jesus to die for my sins. He bathed and cleansed me in his blood. I realized that I could never walk in the fear of the Lord until I released and lost the fear of man. When I placed my life completely at the Lord's feet, I realized the impact of his glory. He released me from those situations where I could now share the beautiful and not-so beautiful parts of me where honesty and purity matter. In Eccl 3:11, truth shines through: "He hath made everything beautiful in his time: also he hath set the world in their heart, so that no man can find out the work that God maketh from the beginning to the end."

Releasing the Outward Man

At this point, I discovered that the greatest hindrance to God's work included the disharmony of my flesh and the inward spirit of God because each tend to go toward opposite directions. I had difficulty submitting to the Holy Spirit's control, thus rendering me incapable of obeying God's highest commands. *Release of the Spirit* by Watchman Nee explains this well:

> Thus we will speak of the inward man as the spirit, the outer man as the soul (thoughts, emotions, and will) and the outermost man as the body. We must know that he who works for God is the one whose inward man can be released. Our spirit seems to be wrapped in a covering so that it can not easily break forth. If we have never learned how to release our inward man by breaking through the outward man, we are not able to serve. Whether our works are fruitful or not depends upon whether our outward man has been broken by the Lord, so that our inward man can pass through that brokenness and come forth.[12]

Breaking the Alabaster Box

God reminded me often that if the alabaster box is not broken, the pure spikenard could not flow forth. I had to be broken to show forth the true Cynthia. I finally understood what God did through all my circumstances. Watchman Nee said it perfectly in *Release of the Spirit*:

> Yet here is our difficulty: we fret over trifles, we

---

12 Watchman Nee, *Release of the Spirit* (Cloverdale, Indiana: Sure Foundation, 1965), 10–13.

murmur at small losses. The Lord is preparing a way to use us, yet scarcely has His hand touched us when we feel unhappy, even to the extent of quarreling with God and becoming negative in our attitude. Brokenness is the way of blessing, the way of fragrance, the way of fruitfulness, but it is also a path sprinkled with blood. Yes, there is blood from many wounds. Experiences, troubles, and trials which the Lord sends us are for our highest good. We cannot expect the Lord to give better things, for these are His best. The Lord employs two different ways to break our outward man; one is gradual, the other sudden. The timing is in His hands. We cannot shorten the time though we can certainly prolong it, by our opinions, our ways, our cleverness, our self-love, our all.[13]

Prayer

My prayer remains that everyone sees the hand of God. Second, I pray his love shines from the realization of what he has done in my life. God sent his son Jesus to die and set all free from sin. Accepting Jesus as Savior is the only pathway to God, and joy abounds in the presence of God.

---

13 Watchman Nee, *Release of the Spirit* (Cloverdale, Indiana: Sure Foundation, 1965), 12–15.

A Journey of Brokenness

Brokenness continues to be a journey. There will be many times in one's life when one must come to God's throne and allow him to work in one's heart. This allows God to delete the unnecessary aspects of life. However, during this time, God holds tight and gives extra love as one accepts his plans. A new song can then come forth, as it did for me. God purged a large chunk of brokenness when he opened up the door of marriage and a new beginning in Canada. Two Scriptures that reflect what God affected in my life include:

- "They prevented me in the day of my calamity: but the LORD was my stay. He brought me forth also into a large place: he delivered me, because he delighted in me" (2 Sm 22:19–20).

- "It is of the Lord's mercies that we are not consumed, because his compassions fail not. They are new every morning: great is thy faithfulness. The Lord is my portion, saith my soul; therefore will I hope in him. The LORD is good unto them that wait for him, to the soul that seeketh him" (Lam 3:22–25).

The Lord showed me his purposes for all the trials:

The various trials have grieved you, but this has brought you to true genuineness and realness. Your hurt has been cleansed, removed, and replaced with compassion and love. My blood creates a place where the evil one cannot penetrate. In me, there is no struggle against any hurt, just my love. I break down the walls and soften hearts. No one will hurt you as long as you continue to follow my ways. I am the only one who takes the hurts and heals by my stripes. Jeremiah 30:17 says, "For I will restore health unto thee, and I will heal thee of thy wounds, saith the LORD."

The wonderful comforter, the Holy Spirit, came who guided me through these trials. When I received the baptism with the Holy Spirit, the veil lifted, and the revelations and gifts of God flowed.

But he that cometh after me is mightier than I, whose shoes I am not worthy to bear: He shall baptize you with the Holy Ghost, and with fire.

Matthew 3:11

CHAPTER SIX
GIFTS OF THE HOLY SPIRIT

Three months after our marriage, George and I visited friends from church. The Lord directed the wife to ask if I had been baptized with the Holy Spirit. I had not, so I accepted the invitation. I grew in leaps and bounds after the baptism and filling with the Holy Spirit. Two weeks later, George and I attended family camp at Living Faith Bible College in Caroline, Alberta. During that week, they gave the invitation to be baptized with the Holy Spirit. I had not spoken in tongues at this point, even though I had the baptism with the Holy Spirit. This turned out to be life-changing. I came home that morning. As my sweetheart made breakfast, I started speaking in tongues and could not stop for twenty minutes.

I can explain tongues as a gift from the Holy Spirit, that is, speaking in another language one has not learned. Many consider tongues as a divine anointed utterance and message from God. Speaking in tongues is the evidence of the Holy Spirit being in control of the individual. This opened the doors to many other gifts from the Holy Spirit, including the interpretation of tongues, that is, making known the saying when one speaks in tongues. Research has shown tongues opens up another part of the brain that normally lacks utilization. In addition, God gave me the gift of prophecy. I started journaling every word God shares each morning. I completed fifteen journals of God's Word. This opened doors for God's direction for our lives. Since the baptism, I also received the gift of discernment, that is, knowing with assurance whether certain behavior is divine, human, or satanic. Several times, God gave visions and word of knowledge regarding situations occurring in other countries. New avenues opened as George watered me with the word of God daily. God reveals much to us as we spend three to six hours daily reading the word of God.

Revelation of God's Word

Prior to this, I did not fully understand the Bible, even after all that education and pursuing my PhD and doctorate in naturology, a science dealing with vitamins and herbs. However, once baptized with the Holy Spirit, I could understand Scriptures. My brain opened full steam ahead as I soaked in all the Scriptures by revelation, not educational knowledge. It appeared as if I had graduated from kindergarten to graduate school in a matter of months. My husband spent many years in the Bible and was amazed at my rapid growth in biblical knowledge. There could not have been any other way to receive these revelations and understanding except by God. I had previously relied on myself, but I found how the human mind remains so limited. God's ways are higher than anyone can imagine. When I do not know what to pray for I remember this verse in Rom 8:26–27: "Likewise the Spirit also helpeth our infirmities: for we know not what we should pray for as we ought: but the Spirit itself maketh intercession for us with groanings which cannot be uttered. And he that searcheth the hearts knoweth what is the mind of the Spirit, because he maketh intercession for the saints according to the will of God."

At the same time, God imparted other gifts. In my thirty-five years in nursing, I saw many healed. Then

God directed me from the medical aspect to natural health. From there, God took me into his presence. As I took his promises of faith, compassion, and laying on of hands, he called me to be utilized as an instrument of his healing. Healing includes everyone. By his stripes, Jesus heals. God chose a healing ministry for my calling. The Holy Spirit took me to a new level of understanding and knowing of God's Word. This inward knowing of God became important as I received revelations through morning devotions, Scriptures, visions, dreams, the words of others, and music. The clarity of the shepherd's voice I can easily distinguish from my own thoughts. All the knowledge I received so far could not compare to the revelations from the Holy Spirit. In *Spiritual Reality or Obsession*, Watchman Nee explains:

> Revelation is the foundation of spiritual progress. Without the revelation of the Holy Spirit no matter how good one's knowledge and how excellent one's outward conduct, that Christian remains superficial before God and may never have advanced even one step forward. On the other hand, if one has a revelation of the Holy Spirit and yet lacks the additional discipline of the Holy Spirit, that Christian's life is incomplete. We may say that the revelation of the Holy Spirit is

the foundation while discipline of the Holy Spirit is the construction. This does not mean that there is a period called revelation of the Holy Spirit and another period called the discipline of the Holy Spirit. The two are mingled. When He reveals, He also disciplines; and when He disciplines, He likewise reveals. For this reason, revelation does not embrace the whole of a Christian's life unless it also includes discipline.[14]

Role of Holy Spirit

The Lord shared, "Do not quench this gift of my love given through the Holy Spirit. This baptism with the Holy Spirit opens up an avenue for revelation of my Word. I bestowed this gift upon you so you could dwell in the spiritual realm. Use this gift wisely, and listen closely."

Circumstances could appear confusing, but the battle takes place in the spiritual realm, not against flesh and blood or individuals. God has the victory and wants each person to be an overcomer in Christ Jesus. The Holy Spirit follows God's will and ways and then leads us to a higher level in the spiritual realm by revealing God's will and plan.

The Holy Spirit gives the counseling, direction, and

---

14 Watchman Nee, *Spiritual Reality or Obsession* (New York: Christian Fellowship Publishers Inc., 1970), 39–40.

guidance for my life on a daily basis. He is the comforter during trying times, disappointments, and mourning. He grieves when I am not in obedience with the word of God. He intercedes when I know not what to pray.

Remember the former things of old: for I am God. And there is none else; I am God, and there is none like me. Declaring the end from the beginning, and from ancient times the things that are not yet done, saying, My counsel shall stand, and I will do all my pleasure.

Isa 46:9–10

Chapter Seven
A New Song

God placed his hand on us from the beginning of our relationship because we placed him first. This God-centered love grew despite the miles apart prior to our marriage. During the preparation for a mission trip to Chile in February, I stood in my kitchen, thinking why not stay in this new home and have George come to the United States. Immediately, I heard a loud voice say, "Are you going to be submissive to your husband?" I knew what this meant. God wanted me to leave country, house, and car and go to Canada to accomplish his will in my life. God's divine destiny continued as we agreed to marry.

So, on April 12, 2005, I boarded the airplane, never

to return to my home again. I embarked on a journey that I could never have imagined. I arrived in Canada to marry George with a one-way ticket and my Maine Coon cat, Rudy. Peace came over me as soon I reached the Canadian border. This peace and joy did not come from the excitement of a new country or new husband, but from finally following God's will. Isaiah 26:3 says, "Thou wilt keep him in perfect peace, whose mind is stayed on thee: because he trusted in thee."

Marriage Covenant

Prior to this, I shipped my belongings separately to my new home in Canada. We began our God-ordained covenant of marriage on April 16, 2005. I had faith because I knew George loved the Lord. This trust stood as I placed all things in God's hands. I looked forward to a good Christian marriage, as it says in Rom 8:28, "And we know that all things work together for good to them that love God, to them who are the called according to his purpose." God now placed me in a real family. The Lord said:

> As a child of the king, you are beautiful and perfect in his sight. My ways are higher than yours are. I bless those who come back to the fold, especially when they have a personal relationship with me. I gave your husband, where

all the passion could be released. I opened your eyes, took off the veil to the superficial love, and opened your eyes to real love. George loves me first in every aspect of his day. I brought you two together to do my will. I connected the passion, the love for me, and your interests in health. I planned this marriage before the foundation of the world. You now walk in my love forever to walk in light and wisdom, accomplish my will, and walk in faithfulness, being the helpmate to your husband. You will walk together in the midst of all circumstances. Waters cannot quench the love for each other because it is my love. You left family, house, and everything to marry and follow my will.

We started our marriage with two Scriptures:

- "But as for me and my house we will serve the Lord" (Jo 24:15).

- "And he hath put a new song in my mouth, even praise unto our God: many shall see it, and fear, and shall trust in the LORD" (Ps 40:3).

Two deer crossed the road as we drove to our wedding. This time, this symbolized the joy of making a true covenant with God. I did not cry during our wedding because my heart remained joyful with God's love. We included in the wedding party all our children who could attend. During the ceremony, we sang "The Worship Song," which continues to press deep in our hearts. This song of praise signifies the basis of our marriage. God placed that song in George's heart so praise would be instilled in our hearts as part of our calling that encourages others to praise.

Blood Covenant

During our honeymoon, God performed a miracle on our wedding night. I am only sharing this sensitive information because of the importance to understand the magnificence of God. God showed me the complete cleansing of my past by literally renewing my virginity. A small amount of blood flowed from the penetrated hymen, like a virgin. The Lord later revealed to me:

> This sign occurred, indicating I cleansed you
> whiter than snow holy and purified by my blood.
> This blood symbolized my covenant with you two.
> This threefold cord can never be broken. I gave
> you this revelation to share with others that, no
> matter what, one can be cleansed by the blood of
> Jesus and transformed by the renewing of one's
> mind as in Rom 12:2: "And be not conformed to
> this world: but be ye transformed by the renewing

of your mind, that ye may prove what is that good, and acceptable, and perfect, will of God." Some may say miracles do not happen today. I want everyone to know I do miracles for everyone in different ways. I melded you two together as one, as I want for all marriages.

God's Favor

Two days after our honeymoon, we arrived at Customs to claim my belongings. Customs required the completion of the immigration process before they could release the boxes. So we immediately proceeded to complete the paperwork. Within two days, we returned to Customs and showed them that we sent the immigration papers. They hesitated, but they realized that meant storing everything for a year and a half. God's favor prevailed. After a few moments of conversation, they agreed to deliver the belongings.

Faith without Works Is Dead

Afterwards, we started our marriage by attending a couples' retreat at Living Faith Bible College. We remained an extra week as part of a workweek and additional honeymoon. We spent that week painting the gym. During this time, the Lord shared this verse in Luke 18:29: "Verily I say unto you, There is no man who has left house, or parents, or brethren, or wife, or children, for the kingdom of God's sake, Who shall not receive manifold more in this present time, and in the world to come life everlasting."

We painted together on many other jobs, which gave us the time together and opportunity to get to know each other. I asked the Lord to shine light upon our gifts so they would blossom to their full potential. This became a real opportunity to learn my role as my husband's helpmate. I pursued several career opportunities, but the Lord said not to work, not even in a nursing career. At first, this seemed difficult. I felt I could not use my gifts to full potential as a housewife. With God's direction, I began to see how being a wife needed to be my first priority. This gave us an opportunity to fully blossom in our relationship. Working would have taken the time needed to build our relationship with God, each other, and our calling.

Commitment beyond Marriage

We sensed the necessity to make a commitment beyond our marriage covenant. We listened to God's voice and took on praise in all circumstances. God said:

> It is time to make a commitment. The doors remain open. I cleansed you. Behold the Lamb of God. You must have spiritual perception before you hear my voice. The spiritual perception will

show you that the hurts from prior years will be healed in minutes or days. The place of pain will be replaced by my reign. The second door is not the door of confession of sin, but the confession of faith by praise and thanks to God. Praise and thank me, and receive my healing. Pray without ceasing. It is time for me to release the seeds of fragrance. Plant yourselves deep in my spirit. Gird up for victory.

Consecration

During our first months of marriage, we also discovered we had to truly consecrate to God. This is a step beyond commitment. Consecration involves a place where one sometimes has to stand separate to complete God's will. I thought I completed all brokenness. God took us deeper into our calling and gave us a new song and a transformed spirit. As I read *Release of the Spirit* by Watchman Nee, his words truly reflected the process God took us through:

> For the outward man to be broken, a full consecration is imperative. Yet we must understand that this crisis act alone will not solve our whole problem in service. Consecration is merely an expression of our willingness to be in the hands of God, and it can take place in just a few minutes. Do not think that God can finish

His dealings with us in this short time. Though we are willing to offer ourselves completely to God, we are just starting on the spiritual road. It is like entering the gate. After consecration, there must be a discipline of the Holy Spirit, this is the pathway. It takes consecration and discipline of the Holy Spirit to make us vessels fit for the Master's use. Without consecration, the Holy Spirit encounters difficulty in disciplining us. Yet consecration cannot serve as a substitute for His discipline. Here then is a vital distinction: our consecration can only be according to the measure of our spiritual insight and understanding, but the Holy Spirit disciplines according to His own light. He orders our circumstances in such a way as to bring about the breaking of the outward man. Since the Holy Spirit works according to the light of God, His discipline is thorough and complete. We often wonder at the things which befall us, yet if left to ourselves we may be mistaken in our very best choice. The discipline He orders transcends our understanding. How often we are caught unprepared and conclude that surely such a drastic thing is not our need.[15]

---

15 Watchman Nee, *Release of the Spirit* (Cloverdale, Indiana: Sure Foundation, 1965), 57–58.

Reconciliation to God

The Lord continued to reveal:

> You two have been obedient. As you pursued
> individual devotions, you heard my voice and
> received revelation. I appointed you keeper of
> my will and your husband keeper of my Word.
> Praise me in the dark places, and my light shines
> brightly. You two must first reconcile to me by
> my Holy Spirit because I made you in my image.
> I made you two one. Reconcile yourselves in one
> body to me through the cross. You cannot forward
> the reconciliation of the people of Israel unto
> me until you reconcile yourselves unto me. Then
> allow my Holy Spirit infilling and die to self. Stay
> in the knowledge of my character. Speak to the
> dry bones that keep you from your restoration
> and reconciliation. Listen to my divine plan for
> your restoration and reconciliation. 2 Corinthians
> 5:18–20 says, "And all things are of God, who
> hath reconciled us to himself by Jesus Christ, and
> hath given to us the ministry of reconciliation;
> To wit, that God was in Christ, reconciling the
> world unto himself, not imputing their trespasses
> unto them; and hath committed unto us the word
> of reconciliation. Now then we are ambassadors

for Christ, as though God did beseech you by us: we pray you in Christ's stead, be ye reconciled to God." This refining process requires purity, holiness, boldness, and faithfulness. I released everything not of me and filled you with my love and Holy Spirit. I desire no backup plans. You must know that radical discipleship is radical obedience. You acquired this teaching as I took off the chaff and the dross. You will fear and tremble for all the prosperity I give. I rescue the most unlovely and those desperately wicked and give them wisdom. Then it remains one's choice to come back into the fold or accept me as Savior. I welcome all who come. I chose you two, not only because of being willing and available, but you understand that you broke every commandment in your heart. As the restorer and reconciler, you understand the vital key to my will involves yielding daily.

Prior to our marriage, God shared we would have two children, Jacob and Deborah. I thought these might be human miracle children. He revealed his plans for Jacob at the Bible study in Hobbema First Nations Reserve in Alberta and Deborah as the repairer of the breach and reconciliation of Israel. We did not understand this in the beginning, but God continues to reveal and unfold his plans.

Hobbema First Nations

God sanctified, consecrated, and set us apart for our calling. God appointed as our first assignment to lay siege spiritually on Hobbema First Nations Reserve. We took authority over the town as watchmen on the wall and interceded continually with prayer. The Bible study progressed over several months. During this time, two received the baptism with the Holy Spirit and one water baptism. They had already accepted Jesus as their Savior prior to the Bible study. The Lord said, "I consecrate this home as a lighthouse where I open eyes and allow my light to continually shine." We drove around the reserve, placing the blood of Jesus and sending ministering angels to each home. God asked us to place the blood of Jesus on the county. Then, over a three-week time period, we placed the blood of Jesus on all the nations throughout the world through prayer as God revealed the specific needs of each nation.

God's Direction

I began to hear God's heart and his direction for our lives. I would journal daily what God said to us. Habakkuk 2:2–3 reflects this process perfectly:

And the Lord answered me, and said, Write the vision, and make it plain upon tables, that he may run that readeth it. For the vision is yet for an appointed time, but at the end it shall speak, and not lie: though it tarry, wait for it; because it will surely come, it will not tarry.

I also recorded the daily miracles and rhema word, a quickened word from God that is spoken or from a Scripture that gives an impression that goes deep into an individual's spirit.

Blood Covenant of Communion

A few months later, God guided and directed us to partake of daily communion. This obedience transformed our lives, which resulted in additional spiritual revelations. As we share daily communion, we recognize God's all sufficiency, the imperativeness of forgiveness to remain healthy, and the necessity of love, first for him, each other, family, and, lastly, our ministry and others. To hear his voice requires holiness and purity. Then sanctification and consecration by his blood allows his grace and mercy to flow. God shared, "I have consecrated the bread and blood, placing healing and forgiveness in your heart. When you partake of communion, this strengthens my love within you. Then I can work my divine purpose and open up my will."

Releasing Idols

God also dealt with idols. Tearfully, I released things from the past. I did not realize I transported so many idols to Canada. God said, "I had you bring them so you two could release the idols together." I had pictures, clothing, and gifts from past relationships. The Holy Spirit worked in my heart as I released everything that God had not purposed for our calling which included attachments. This continued for several weeks. Then God unveiled our eyes and said, "I am asking you to release everything with images (pictures, ceramics, clothing, and jewelry). This comes from the path I chose for you, not legalism." In Deut 7:25, it states, "The graven images of their gods shall ye burn with fire: thou shalt not desire the silver or gold that is on them, nor take it unto thee, lest thou be snared therein: for it is an abomination to the LORD thy God." The release continued as we realized our calling required a narrow path.

Submission

One of the greatest lessons I needed to learn required submission, the key to the open door of wisdom. Ephesians 5:22 says, "Wives submit yourselves unto your own husbands, as unto the Lord." Independent and doing my own thing, I failed to realize what it required to submit. I knew the Scripture prior to marriage. I assumed this would not be difficult to submit this time because I knew that, when one submits to one's husband, one submits to God. But my will rose up often, which I released to the Lord. Words may be downloaded, but the fruit of God's Word cannot be seen, but instilled by the Holy Spirit. I realized my husband and I stood on equal ground, but I have a different role as a wife. Neither role requires a superior position, exactly like the Trinity. The Godhead (God, Jesus, and Holy Spirit) remain equal in power and in substance, but each has a different function. Submission, a position willingly assumed in obedience to Jesus, necessitates an attitude of humility. In submission, one places another first rather than looking after one's own interests. The world tells about the foolishness of submission and how one loses power, but the Scripture tells how submission gives one access to the power and protection of God.

There is another aspect to submission. A woman wants love; a man wants respect. Finally loved, I trust my husband because he places God first, and his priority bears fruit of a God-centered marriage. But my independent nature gave input more than once. My husband wanted to know his ideas maintained validity and viewed this repeated input as disrespect. In addition, because we had limited dating prior to our marriage, we needed to know each other. We have now come to a great place of transparency. God desires this transparency for all marriages.

One of the aspects of following a life of Christ is to follow the spiritual, not the flesh. The flesh may rise up and say, "What is going on?" I want my way, but the submission of the Father says we should stay focused on his will. Then one's calling becomes clear. Give to others and not the world. Then the world will become strangely dim. One then remains in the spiritual realm, not the natural realm.

Releasing the Chaff and Dross

At the same time, God continues to reveal more as we read the word of God three to six hours a day, which includes a daily study of the Word. He took off the chaff and dross as we released our comfort zone. God disrupted the comfort zone as we released control and gave up criticizing others who held different opinions. When one speaks the truth in love and allows the Holy Spirit to complete his work, the comfort zone becomes easier to release. At this same time, the Lord told us to downsize. We proceeded to downsize the furniture and gave the antiques to our children. We gave away the master bedroom furniture and slept in the spare room in preparation for the move to Ottawa. This process took a period of two years. The Lord spoke, "As you downsize, you place your treasures in me and not the world." Fasting helped to press through all these issues. God shared when to fast, specifying the type of fast he required. Some fasts included three days of liquids only, three days of water, or fasting from television and computer. The importance of entertainment decreases as we occasionally watch the news.

One of the most difficult times occurred when I gave up my nursing license. God said I could not go between two opinions. At this point, I had not worked in the nursing field for two years. A tug remained in my flesh to give up the nursing license because nursing had been my identity for thirty-five years. However, I knew this could be a backup plan. God had another plan for my life, as I released my license.

After the Lord took away the chaff and dross, we continued to see the daily process of coming to the cross and dying to self by allowing God to reign in our daily decisions. This true relationship with Jesus remains a continual journey. When my flesh appears strong, I am reminded of the Scripture in Prov 3:5, "Trust in the Lord with all thine heart; and lean not unto thine own understanding." I realized that, as finely as the snowflakes are created, this is how fine God has removed the chaff and dross.

Releasing the Comfort Zone

The flesh likes to be comfortable. One day, the Lord said:

> Come out of your comfort zone. Be bold and
> courageous because I position and posture you
> to propel my purposes. Remember that status
> quo does not serve me. Your destiny to surround,
> nurture, and protect has you stand in the gap
> for Israel. Knit my people together for the
> reconciliation. I seat you two in my victory. Lift
> yourselves up boldly in my strength. You have the
> authority and know that, when two agree, your
> prayers make a difference for individuals as well
> as nations. Create waves, and then ride them.
> I will complete the good work I started. Know
> that withholding serves no purpose because your
> charisma must be shown to the world and be fully
> expressed.

Seeking new horizons out of our comfort zone has been an important step of obedience to his will. Most people have a routine and feel uncomfortable in treading new territories. Releasing the comfort zone is critical to come into the boldness needed to complete God's will.

Putting on the Whole Armor of God

Another important part of the last couple years of our marriage that cannot be overemphasized is daily putting on the whole armor of God to stand in the will of the Lord and prevent attacks from the evil one through thoughts. One needs to receive as much education as one possibly can. Nevertheless, one quickly discovers, education will not help in the fight with the unseen spiritual enemies. In these times, one moves beyond fleshly defense and utilizes the spiritual armor, which empowers one to successfully stand against the evil one.

- **Belt of Truth**

The first part of the armor is the belt of truth. This requires openness and honesty with yourself and others, especially in marriage, so no secrets hide in dark places. This is a holy place of transparency and safety where everything can be shared allowing us to pray for one another.

- **Breastplate of Righteousness**

God also deals with the breastplate of righteousness by keeping one free from condemnation, false accusations, and guilty thoughts. When one dresses in righteousness, one takes on the Lord Jesus Christ, and his light radiates to others. This happened when I released all the shame of my past and followed God's way.

- **Shoes of Peace**

I put on the shoes of peace when I came to Canada. I no longer experienced the hostility inside as I did God's will. Also, a peace remains there daily. Colossians 3:15 says, "Let the peace of God rule in your hearts." There is no worrying, fretting, or anxiety because God is in all circumstances. God's faithfulness shows up as I allow his will in my life.

- **Shield of Faith**

Another aspect of the armor includes the shield of faith. A fresh anointing of the Holy Spirit's presence happens as one saturates in the word of God. Then one can wave the banner of faith, like a shield in the face of the enemy, and every dart falls to the ground. The Lord told us several times that he was about to take us to a higher level. Every time, we apparently had a crack. The evil one would attack over small insignificant things. But the time taken to pull up our shield of faith has decreased.

- **Helmet of Salvation**

The helmet of salvation means more than accepting Christ as your personal Savior. This means taking captive every thought and imagination, replacing fear with faith, and releasing strongholds. This became evident as I gained victory from the fear of rejection of past relationships. I stood in faith and came to Canada to marry, leaving the strongholds of the past behind and obtaining a healthy relationship. We did not falter and stood up in faith to move to Ottawa.

- **Sword of the Spirit**

The word of God, the sword of the Spirit, remains our strength. This gives us the ability to remember or find a Scripture quickly when situations arise where we need refreshing. The sword is two-edged. The one edge is where the Word comes out of God's mouth as we read the Bible. The other edge is when the word of God comes out of our mouth. So, when we are confronted, God's Word comes out of our mouth to defeat the enemy, edify, and go deeply into the spirit of another person. It cuts through one's thoughts and emotion. In other words, it cuts through the soul and goes to the spirit of the individual. Our life is no longer about our plans, but about God's plans.

Transformation of My Thoughts on Healing

Now was a good time to continue my doctorate and PhD. However, because these degrees did not appear relevant to my calling, it would be quite important to ask

God about completing these courses. He made it clear he wanted me to finish for these three purposes:

1. The dissertation, "Faith for Healing," with the premise that healing is a present promise from God that one appropriates by faith[16]

2. The credibility in writing my testimony

3. God's use of healthy eating, exercise, natural herbs, and vitamins to heal the body

God does not call me to set up practice. Although, where opportunities arise, I share information for healing.

Journey to Israel

On November 17, 2005, the Lord told us to go to Israel and pray daily for the peace of Jerusalem. Within a period of a few months, God worked in our hearts and gave us a passion for Israel. The Lord revealed the following, "Before the holy journey to Israel, I placed a yearning to see Israel in your heart. I wanted you to visit my chosen land and interact with my people." On March 12, 2007, this holy journey became a reality. God designed this as a holy journey, not just a tour. The holy journey included seventeen people. God handpicked each individual. We

---

16 The dissertation is available on our Web site, knowledge2revelation.com.

did not have the money for the journey. God provided. First, our daughter paid for the airline ticket from Edmonton, Alberta, to Newark, New Jersey. We spent time with my two sisters, who met my husband for the first time. We placed the remainder on credit at God's direction, not his usual way of provision. We believed God's promise, and God completely paid the credit card. I will always remember this holy time as we journeyed all over Israel and Jordan and walked in the steps of Jesus.

God's Rainbow Covenant and Anointing

As we drove just above the Jordan River to be baptized in the midst of a cold, rainy day, a beautiful rainbow appeared. The rainbow is the token of the covenant God made with Noah that God would never again flood the whole Earth. Genesis 9:13–15 says, "I do set my bow in the cloud, and it shall be for a token of a covenant between me and the earth. And it shall come to pass, when I bring a cloud over the earth, that the bow shall be seen in the cloud: And I will remember my covenant, which is between me and you and every living creature of all flesh; and the waters shall no more become a flood to destroy all flesh."

The sky cleared, and the weather suddenly turned warm. The Lord made the anointing in the Jordan River a special covenant, demonstrated by the appearance of the rainbow. Before we left for Israel, God directed us to dip in the Jordan River seven times, which was the anointing for our calling. Interestingly, both our tour guides stood on either side of us to assist as we dipped in the Jordan River.

Healing and Miracles

A few days later, we walked down to the Dead Sea, where I severely sprained my ankle. My ankle became swollen and bruised. In the natural realm, how would I walk in Jerusalem for the next five days? Faith rose up, and I knew God brought me to Israel to see Jerusalem. This required continual walking for the remainder of the journey. An inner knowing came forth to have others on the tour lay hands on my ankle. Twelve came to the room, laid hands on my ankle, and prayed. The next day, the tour guide brought a wheelchair, expecting I would not be able to walk. I did not need the wheelchair because I appropriated my faith. The next morning, without pain, God's miracle prevailed as I walked to breakfast, even though my foot continued to be swollen and bruised. In fact, I walked five miles that day in Jerusalem and five miles each of the remaining five days. The total tour involved sixty miles of walking.

The miracles that happened in Israel also occur today in North America. This faith lesson happened as I prayed his will and allowed God to not only heal, but for others to actually see the miracle. Another miracle happened during the journey as two people in the tour group married six months later. Even the tour guide exclaimed how God chose the people already in the spiritual realm and wanted a touch on a deeper level. What great things God does when individuals seek his face. In this season, as one seeks God's guidance, he gives a higher plan that far exceeds our expectations. My love and heart remain for his chosen people of Israel. I realized God's presence on a greater level than at home because North America has much covetousness, greed, and idols. As I returned, he unveiled my eyes and showed me the idols as well as all the facets of my masks.

Shaking of the Earth and Everyone's Spirit

God shared with us that he would shake every idol by shaking the whole Earth as in Ezekiel's prophesies in chapters 38 and 39. God shared:

> As I shake the whole earth, I remove the prison
> bars and shake the foundation of all souls,
> loosening all the chains. This shaking far exceeds
> the quake that Paul and Silas experienced because
> many individuals will be saved and freed. I grieve
> for those who hold others prisoners because of
> the hurts. All will see my ways and come to me.

This shaking will not only shake the Earth, but I will shake the inner spirits of every individual. This will come at a time you least expect. I have sent ministering angels ahead to minister to each individual for the preparation. This world will never be the same. I do not leave my people without provision. Did I not provide for the people of Israel for forty years? I want many more to accept me, Jesus, as Savior before I return.

The Calling on Our Life

In 2007, God told us to move to Ottawa with the promise of a thousand square-feet suite. We found this suite over the Internet in June 2008. We knew that, even before we saw the place, God designed this suite for us if they were agreeable. They e-mailed back, "We are agreeable." That's all that they wrote in the e-mail. After the agreement, we discovered the home address appeared to be in Gatineau, Quebec, not Ottawa, Ontario. We asked the Lord, "You said our place was in Ottawa but it is actually in Quebec. Did we hear you correctly? " The Lord responded, "Yes, I want you in metro Ottawa. You will minister to the natives in Quebec, learn French, and work with the legislators in Ottawa. I placed you here for your two-year internship with me. I will then send you to all the nations to spread the gospel and minister, including a healing ministry. This will be complete with three and a half years in Israel, the final destiny of your calling."

Faith for God's Provision

God gave provision for the trip by the gift of money received from the church, sale of our appliances, and yard sale. God promised four months earlier that after our truck sold, he would give us the 1990 Cadillac we had viewed. The day before we left for Ottawa, our miracle manifested. We had the car in the Elias name. God gives good gifts to his children. Our faith increased as we went through times where we received provision just in time for needed food. We depended on the Lord as we sowed seed. God shared, "I have given you two my provision. At times, you had a few dollars. Other times, you had nothing. I provided the food and paid off your Israel journey. I also provided money from your 1978 car with the faulty electrical system and an unexpected gift from the church to pay the bills. Your mustard seed faith increased, as does my provision. You have come to know my character of majesty, mercy, grace, meekness, justice, faithfulness, provider, healer, and much more."

During these times of lack, we fully realized the importance of Deut 8:3: "Man doth not live by bread only, but by every word that proceedeth out of the mouth of the LORD doth man live."

The Holy Journey

As we proceeded on our holy journey in the first week of September 2008 to Ottawa, Quebec, our car broke down in Provost, Alberta. Two paramedics stopped and called for a tow truck, a father-and-son operation. The paramedics said, "You are in good hands. The dad is the best mechanic in the country, and he will have you going." The mechanic worked on the car until midnight on Saturday. Then they took us to church on Sunday. Afterwards, they invited us for dinner and several other meals. As we prepared to leave, we noticed the U-Haul lights did not work. This repair took several additional hours. God told us, "Without this, you could have been in a serious accident or stopped by the police for no lights. I had ten thousand angels protecting my anointed ones. The full extent of my will manifested as you prayed for reuniting of their church and the healing of their hemophiliac sons. I healed the church and the family who professed my love with their good deeds. Then, the next day, my angels came alongside you again as you ran out of gas. A car stopped and sent their son with gas, which they gave without cost."

Dying to Self

God taught us a lesson in dying to self. We apparently lost track of time and thought we had arrived in Quebec on Friday, but it was actually Saturday. We worked the next day, Sunday, cleaning. Then the next day, actually Monday, we drove to the church, where we found the doors locked except for the office. When we entered the office, they told us it happened to be Monday, not Sunday. What could we say? We had earlier requested for God to place us where we had no way out, but to die to self. That opportunity arrived. This part of our internship left us without masks to cover, face to save, or words to dispute. God gives lessons like these from the beginning to the end of life.

Perfect Place of Worship

God revealed he had the perfect place of worship for us in Ottawa. He then directed us to a second church full of truth and the Holy Spirit. This experience took us to Peace Tower Church, where we ascertained God wanted us to attend because they had the heart for Israel as God placed in our hearts.

The Lord wanted us to attend another church the third week. Surprised, we went with an open heart, but that church lacked the Holy Spirit infilling. We realized the Lord sent us to teach us the lesson of faith. We had difficulty with the directions and drove twenty minutes out of the way. We started to revamp our directions. The next thing we knew, we approached the correct exit. This seemed impossible until we realized God had transported us to the exit. Our mustard seed faith increased.

Finally, God verified Peace Tower as our home church and home base. Elated, we knew God planted us here during our two-year internship in Ottawa before ministering to the nations and then Israel. At this point, a friend said, "Wow! You received everything through the Internet." Then we realized that God utilized the Internet to find each other, our home in Gatineau, and now our church home. Within a few weeks of attending Peace Tower Church, Jesus healed my husband of tinnitus, ringing in the ears. We continue to praise the Lord for each moment he designs.

Rejoice evermore. Pray without ceasing. In everything give thanks for this is the will of God in Christ Jesus concerning you.

1 Thess 5:16–18

CHAPTER EIGHT
PRAISE

Praise became an essential part of our life. It started with the praise song, "The Worship Song," we sang during our wedding ceremony. Praise grew from there as we read all Merlin Carothers' books on praise. My husband already experienced the power of praise but I did not realize the power of praise prior to our marriage. One very powerful statement from the book *Prison to Praise* that I claim includes:

> Jesus didn't promise to change the circumstances around us, but He did promise great peace and pure joy to those who would learn to believe that God actually controls all things. The very act of praise releases the power of God into a set of

circumstances and enables God to change them if this is His design. Very often it is our attitudes that hinder the solution of a problem. God is sovereign and could certainly cut across our wrong thought patterns and attitudes. But His perfect plan is to bring each of us into fellowship and communion with Him, and so He allows circumstances and incidents which will bring our wrong attitudes to our attention. I have come to believe that the prayer of praise is the highest form of communion with God, and one that always releases a great deal of power into our lives. Praising Him is not something we do because we feel good; but rather an act of obedience. Often the prayer of praise is done in sheer teeth-gritting willpower; yet when we persist in it, somehow the power of God is released into us and into the situation. At first in a trickle perhaps, but later in a growing stream that finally floods us and washes away the old hurts and scars.[17]

Praise Means Trusting God

When we first married, I would say "Praise the Lord" for many things, even though I did not feel like praising the Lord. But, as time went on, I saw my attitude changing

17 Merlin Carothers, Prison to Praise (Escondido, California: Merlin Carothers, 2004), 91–92.

when I praised. I began to see the power of trusting God in everything. I am blessed with peace and love in our marriage. Nevertheless, I found praise worked when I would praise God for a malfunctioning computer or broken dishes. I praise God even in the little things.

True Test of Praise

Then, one day, the true test came. We lived in Ottawa about a month when our son called and told us he had a brain tumor. After the call, my husband and I immediately got down on our knees and praised the Lord for his will and what he was going to effect through all of this. We believed for a total wholeness and healing. When we praised God and prayed his will, he revealed that he healed our son in a way that would affect the whole family, district, and church. We had total peace as we asked many for prayer. This continues to be a total trust in God. He views praise not as a bargaining tool or a place of denial, but as a place to trust, no matter what the circumstance. God has a reason for everything. He works everything out for good for those who love God. It may not look good as one experiences difficulty. But one can later see how God works it out for his glory. I look forward with excitement to the journey not yet taken.

The following is a praise poem my husband wrote:

Praise

Praise is the power that answers your prayers

As you lay upon Jesus the load of your cares

Even when your balance is low at the banks

The Lord will supply as you give and say thanks

When aches and pains make you go so slow

Praise is the answer for your get-up-and-go

When disappointments come and you want to give up

Praise from your lips will put you on top

So if you want to be a winner in every way

Be sure to give praise to God all day

George Elias

I send thee to the children of Israel, to a rebellious nation that hath rebelled against me: they and their fathers have transgressed against me, even to this very day.

Ezek 2:3

Chapter Nine
Vision of the Journey
Not Yet Taken

The Revelation of Our Calling

The doors will open up in Ottawa and Quebec these next couple years with the calling of God to work with the legislators in Ottawa, the natives in Quebec, and whatever the Lord directs. We will live in Gatineau for at least two years on an internship with God. Afterwards, Gatineau will continue as our home base as we travel to all the nations.

After the internship, we will be traveling to all the nations sharing the gospel, including a healing ministry. Part of the journey includes traveling to Denmark to share God's view on abortion, especially in regards to

Turner syndrome babies. We will share the gospel, God's true intent for marriage, God's will as in the "Lord's Prayer," communion, praise, and God's presence in all circumstances. We do not know how this will unfold, but we do know we need to remain willing and available. God said he would place people in our path to assist financially. We will eventually end up in Israel as part of the reconciliation of his people of Israel to himself. We eagerly await what God will unfold. At present, the hunters and the fishers work to locate his people to be brought back to the land of Israel, as in Jer 16:16: "Behold I will send for many fishers, saith the LORD, and they shall fish them; and after will I send for many hunters, and they shall hunt them from every mountain, and from every hill, and out of the holes of the rocks."

In 2004, I wrote in my journal:

God tests my faith, and I believe he is preparing me for one of the greatest missions of his will. I am to be a wife, as in Prov 31:10–12: "Who can find a virtuous woman? For her price is far above rubies. The heart of her husband doth safely trust in her, so that he shall have no need of spoil. She will do him good and not evil all the days of her life." That transformation will be necessary to do God's will. True importance stands on the fact that my relationship with God remains pristine. Rise up with faith toward the goal of the prize. I am a child of God who rebuilds broken walls and mends the breaches, a true threat to the enemy.

God was speaking to me before meeting my husband about our marriage and our calling as *repairer of the breach.*

Manifestation of Dreams and Visions

The reconciliation of Israel to God will be the manifestation of the dream I had on Oct 10, 2005. I saw many baskets of sheaves. This represented all the people of Israel being reconciled to God. In addition, on November 13, 2005, my husband and I were walking. God showed me a vision and said, "You will see the Mount of Olives, go into all the world, and preach the gospel." We stood on the Mount of Olives in 2007 when we toured Israel. Also, our destiny takes us to the nations to share the gospel, completing the journey in Israel.

God's Destiny for Us

The following are many words that God revealed:

The seed of your destiny is interwoven in your bones. Your seed becomes watered by faith as my Word blossoms into the full goodness of my purposes, which grow into full olive trees to form your destiny. Yielding to me daily is a vital key to this destiny. You two still want part of yourselves to run your destiny. Totally give yourselves to me. Then the floodgates will open. You are cleansed anew. You know my promises and my Word, and you cannot go between the two opinions of fear and faith. So rise up with faith, and give all to walk on high hills. Your boldness comes from the Holy Spirit. I bless you with peace. I cause showers of blessings to come upon you in this season. My olive trees will yield much fruit because I have broken the yoke and the bonds. I make a garden of renown, and all will know I am the Lord. Your dry bones will live again. George will speak my words, and you will shine my love, compassion, and healing on others as they follow my ways. Your passion increases as you discern my desires.

Take the Name God of Jehovah to the Nations

I wrote your name "Elias" literally in the Scriptures. I favored you with a high calling. Depend totally on the Holy Spirit. Take the name Elias, God of Jehovah, to the world with boldness. I choose each name. Most importantly, spread my name, Jesus, and my Word. Know these words are true in Matt 17:11: "Elias truly shall first come, and restore all things. But I say unto you that Elias is come already, and they knew him not, but have done unto him whatsoever they listed. Likewise shall also the Son of man suffer of them." In Mark 9:12, it says, "And he answered and told them, Elias verily cometh first, and restoreth all things; and how it is written of the Son of man, that he must suffer many things, and be set as nought."

The Covenant of the Calling

I gave you two the mantle, sanctification, and impartation for your calling prior to the Holy Journey to Israel. Then you were anointed for your calling in the Jordan River and consecrated on the Mount of Beatitudes. I purified and showed you areas previously impure, divided, and idolatrous. This process exposed jealousy, covetousness, materialism, worship of your own bodies, pride, intellectualism, and lust. I have removed this chaff. Then I refined you in the fire as the potter with the clay and took away the dross. The chaff will not return because I do a perfect work as you continue to reveal your heart to me

God's Footprints on Our Life

Your destiny fulfilled through crisis requires those dead bones to come alive and heal others and for the salvation of my people Israel, all nations, your family, and friends. I placed my footprints on you. Continue to seek my face. I send additional intercessors at the right time. They will be people you do not expect. You need the intercessory covering for your calling, which I consecrated for such a time as this. The blood placed over all nations sets my will in place for the shaking. When you lean not on your own understanding, I can work in all my fullness. Your husband will be known in the gates of the nation of Canada. Listen to my promises. Do not depart to the right or the left.

Watchman on the Wall

As the watchman on the wall for my people, follow my ways, and imprint them in your heart. I use testing to form my character in you. I designed you as a helpmate who can call forth your husband like no other to comfort, encourage, and challenge him with life-giving words. Rely on my strength.

Fear Only God with Faith and Strength

You can no longer take offense as the king's child. Do not fear man, but fear me. Take the power of your faith to heal. Give control to me, and receive my blessings. As you have experienced, anger produces nothing. I gave you the gift of prophesy and healing as the fruit of my love. Your calling cannot be defiled by envy and resentment. Seeking my face requires time in prayer and in the Word and having my Holy Spirit in full power. This involves not your own effort, but my love from the Holy Spirit. I took your shame and gave you double honor. For your sweetheart, I took confusion and gave him double wisdom. I give everlasting joy to you. Your calling requires my faith and strength. Rely only on me. I develop your character to receive my promises, which you receive in proportion to your willingness to wait for my timing. I blessed you with a tongue of love, kindness, and truth. The name Elias does not come without reason, but by a high purpose.

Boldness and Favor

I chose you for a calling exceeding in favor. I cleansed you pure as a shining pearl. Go and reconcile my people to me. I have placed this deep into your hearts. Go forth to all the nations, speak your testimonies before kings, and be not ashamed. My Holy Spirit gives the words. I teach and give you the wisdom of the ages needed to empower you. To believe the truth of what I say, go to war with worship, praise, and faith for the whole world will shake. Intervene for these nations because they will hear me deep within their hearts. Continue to purpose yourselves with a pure heart with my love and sincere faith. Always live life in the context of eternity and in purity and holiness according to your calling. Take inventory of everything; measure each according to your calling. Doubt and unbelief must be ushered out to call in boldness.

My Desires Become God's Desires

Stand in peace, my child. I weigh the heart. You may try to cover your personal flaws with niceness, but they are exposed in your actions and thoughts. I look at the motives. Trust me. This trust will come by yielding to the Holy Spirit and praise. Your emotions and thoughts change like the wind, but know that I know the posture of your heart. Your desires become my desires as I transform your heart to beat in accordance with

mine. Divine destiny requires obedience and faith.
Stand in my ways, and stand again. Take bold
action because I transformed you for my glory.

Pray, Praise, and Worship

I heal the hurts that hurt others. The blessings
unfold as you speak blessings over each other.
My words can heal and accomplish great things.
Your part is to pray, praise, and worship me in all
things. I gave you many gifts to unwrap without
idols and clutter. Prophesy to the dry bones for
new life is happening. Seek the places that hinder
my boldness to shine forth. Go to a higher level,
and stand in the midst of relinquishing your
comfort zone. Know I have things under control.
If you simply do your life to avoid my correction
and watch the clock for each moment of escape,
you fail to recognize the blessings of your calling.
Your marriage came from a dream birthed as small
children.

Many Are Called; Few Are Chosen

I forward your journey and your testimony as a
beginning of my plans. As you continue in my
direction, I manifest great things. I call many,
but I choose few. I have chosen you two for
this assignment because of your willingness and

availability. You gave your hearts to me and stand firm on my promises. I took you several levels in your Christian walk these last three years. I supplied all your needs according to my riches in glory. You released many things, and you experienced how this turned out for your good as you kept my ways and commandments. You have charge over my courts and walk on high hills. Remember that I am the branch. Refrain from digging up unbelief from what you have sown in faith. The Holy Spirit removes the past with cleansing, mercy, and grace. Do not hold to the garbage. Dump it, and drive away. Live in patience, persistence, pliability, and passion without the shame of failure, fear, or generational curse. You have authority to send the evil one to the abyss.

Wisdom and Guidance

I have everything under control from the foundation of the world. Listen for my ways, and allow my will. I guide and direct each step of the way. When you seek my face, you find the answers. Refrain from going off the path of the straight and narrow. Remain faithful that your testimony will be received by my grace to millions. I have a special calling for everyone, but everyone does not hear, or they disregard me. I impact individuals to realize my love and know that I died on the cross for each person. What makes my wisdom difficult to hear? I talk with all individuals through my Holy Spirit, but few listen closely to my words. I kept your husband young for your calling and for you before the foundation of the world. This keeps peace knowing I am in everything. It also forwards prophecy. You will find the heart of those who will send you all over the world and Israel. I am purposing this in someone's heart now. I will even send you into secret meeting places underground, where you will share my word. Be strong and of good courage. Do not fear nor be dismayed because I will not fail or forsake you. Finish the work for my kingdom. Remember that I give you everything. You must know me intimately to present me to others. You will eat, sleep, and be clothed out of my hand with obedience. You have not reached one inch of the praises you will be singing. Much of your prophesying in Israel will be the praising of what I give in the eternal life. I give you visions of the New Jerusalem. I knew that, when I placed you two together as apostle and prophetess, you would come into full power for my glory. Keep the passion for me and each other and my will. You will not accept watered-down versions of the truth. Submerge in my word, and align your life, body, ministry, and marriage with the truth. Refuse to compromise. I entrusted you two with bringing salvation, healing, and deliverance to people in your city, nation, and world through me. You accepted this mission as a living sacrifice, and you remain willing to die for your calling. I will reveal my total will in the fullness of time.

Release of the Calling

I release you to these Scriptures:

- "For God hath not given us a spirit of fear; but of power, and of love, and of a sound mind" (2 Tm 1:7).

- "Who hath saved us, and called us with an holy calling, not according to our works, but according to his own purpose and grace, which was given us in Christ Jesus before the world began" (2 Tm 1:9).

- "Now the God of peace ... Make you perfect in every good work to do his will, working in you that which is well pleasing in his sight, through Jesus Christ; to whom be glory for ever and ever. Amen" (Heb 13:20–21).

Reconciliation of Israel

I am preparing you physically and spiritually to ensure the reconciliation of Israel. Allow my love to transform your life like a drink offering. Then those who cannot comprehend will see the light in you two as an everlasting passion that is spread throughout the whole Earth. I purpose to redeem a multitude from every nation, tribe, and tongue, no matter the cost. Do not be deterred by internal or external fires because I have placed my love, which needs to be shared throughout all nations. I created the inner sanctuary of the temple as sacred, and the boundaries cannot be broken. I gather my remnant of Israel and gather them altogether, like sheep unto the fold. They will pass through the gate, and I will be their head as I restore and show my glory. As you reconcile Israel, do not feel alone. Look at Esther, who forsook the pressure of the whole world and saved her people from destruction. Rejoice in me and the God of your salvation. Ask and you will be given. Seek and you will find. Knock and it will be opened. People will know you two by your fruits. You two have built your home on the rock. There remains a justification of my truth, beauty, and wisdom. I took you from the pits of destruction and placed you together for your destiny.

Mandate of My Healing Ministry

The hands that touched unclean things will now heal. What I have cleansed, no one can call unclean. Your faith and trust in me is vital. Trusting in man leads to strength in flesh and not strength in spirit. As you consider your destiny, fly with wings of eagles. As you continually repent, come into my throne room. I choose few to come into the inner holies. You have buried the deep sensitivity because you could not bear to carry it yourself. I bear the burden. The dry bone of sensitivity will rise up and know my love and compassion. I want you to crusade the message of the gospel, praise, marriage, and so forth. This crusade is beyond anything you could comprehend, starting with my lighthouse in Hobbema and continuing in Ottawa. I give you a confirmation and show my strength. Gird up

your armor. You will be more like me in the next
year and will not recognize yourselves. I love you
more than you can comprehend. Wait patiently.
In due time, you will gather up the crop and the
harvest. Take and plant new seedlings in Israel
and the world. Share the light like a candle. My
power will open up like a bonfire. Listen as I use
you as a fine and beautiful instrument. Go in
my way and power so my glory shines. You will
be used to heal millions. Your desire to bring
wellness and to transform health will come about
far differently than expected. Take bold action as
you receive direction. Act on what I commission.
Then I perform miracles. Accept the new identity
I give as healer and prophetess. I am the great
physician. You will be used to heal by my stripes.
Mother Teresa wept with compassion and love
and ministered as a repairer of the breach. I want
you to continue, but in a different way. I created
your love and passion for seniors that only they
understand. Reach them for time is short. I anoint
you to heal and lay hands on the sick. You must
appropriate the healing even when symptoms
remain. This means seeing the healing with
spiritual eyes. You will also cast out the evil spirits
and discern spirits through my grace. The years

prior to your marriage, you used your skills as a nurse and CEO with your kindness, love, and compassion to heal others. Now I anoint you as an instrument to heal others through my divine healing.

Afterword

I praise God for how he transformed my life—not to religion, but to faith in Jesus. The way to your transformation is to first accept Jesus as Savior by saying the prayer at the end of the conclusion. Then find fellowship with other Christians in a church setting or a home. One thing important to be addressed is deliverance from ungodly lifestyles. This can be done immediately, or you may need to seek someone credible to assist you. The baptism by immersion and baptism with the Holy Spirit then leads to the necessary boost to take you from fear to faith. Fear can leave you unable to fulfill your full potential. Your faith, although small as a mustard seed, can be used to leap into spiritual growth. Only in the covenant blood of Jesus can your true destiny be fulfilled.

Conclusion

God's mercy and graciousness did not leave me untouched. He continually works in my heart to draw me closer to him. I continually praise God for my life transformation and key to eternity. I am strengthened daily by his will for my life. This occurs by and accepting God's will and dying to self daily. When I share and allow transparency, the truth comes to light. God permeates every fiber of my being. When I praise, that says I trust him. When I repent, he places me in his peace, joy, and grace. God remains my refuge in all circumstances. Without those difficult circumstances, how could I have known God's love? The blood of Jesus covers all. I learned that all the educational knowledge was minuscule compared to the revelations received from God. It is time to rise up and release my passion for the calling of God. My passion is for Israel. I am a living testimony of John 8:36: "If the Son therefore shall make you free, ye shall be free indeed." With the past complete, I now live in freedom. I also look forward to God's will for my future. I now realize how to fight the spiritual battle, not against others or myself, but against the evil one. My journey in *From Knowledge to Revelation* is summed up in one verse, "And you shall know the truth, and the truth shall make you free" (Jn 8:32).

In retrospect, my life started out as a good little girl with God hovering over me and keeping me from permanent disasters. Born with Turner syndrome, God gave me a scholarly mind that would take me through to a master's in nursing, an MBA, and a doctorate and PhD in naturology. At fifteen, a collision with a car while riding my bike could have been fatal had God not intervened and lessened the impact. Now God is omnipotent, omniscient, and omnipresent, but, unlike Superman, he does not pull us out of every difficult or dangerous spot. He will not go against our will, so I jumped into the first marriage against my parent's better judgment. God was still there. This marriage started me on the road away from God and into abuse, reconciliation, swinging, and finally divorce. Pursuing my education the next six years took me to another offer. I jumped into marriage again, only wanting love, but looking to the wrong one and not realizing God has all the love we need. Divorced again and blurting out that a woman would be a better mate brought the opportunity for a lesbian relationship, which formed in a commitment where, once again, God appeared through his Holy Spirit with me weeping uncontrollably, stumbling to the floor, and not realizing God was also weeping for me.

Finally, things went my way as CEO of my own business until God showed up, stepped in, and had me arrested. I did not recognize God, not here or in any previous situations. When he got through, God took the business, my mate, and my income. During this time, an invitation came to go to church. Again, God revealed himself as my loving Father. He forgave me, placed his arms around me, cleansed me, and directed me into his will. Now I have peace, freedom, a loving husband, the greatest marriage in the world, God's provision, and the greatest calling for my life. My past, with all its opportunities and accomplishments, remains like a dot beside a basketball in comparison to what I have now. God, my loving Father, was available all the time, but I did not know. I now have total freedom in the covenant blood of Jesus Christ. I want to assure you that God is always in your life, waiting to place his loving arms around you to forgive you, deliver you, and welcome you into the family of God. So, no matter who you are or what your situation, turn to God wherever you are, as you are, and pray this prayer:

LORD JESUS,

I believe you died for me and God raised you from the dead.

Forgive all my sins, and take all my sins away.

Come into my heart, be my Savior and Lord, and fill me with your Holy Spirit.

Amen.

Promises

- **Health:** "And the prayer of faith shall save the sick, and the Lord shall raise him up; and if he have committed sins, they shall be forgiven him" (Jas 5:15).

- **Finances:** "But my God shall supply all your need according to his riches in glory by Christ Jesus" (Phil 4:19).

- **Deliverance:** "The angel of the LORD encampeth round about them that fear him, and delivereth them" (Ps 34:7).

- **Repentance:** "I say unto you, that likewise joy shall be in Heaven over one sinner that repenteth, more than over ninety and nine just persons, which need no repentance" (Lk 15:7).

- **Healing:** "But he was wounded for our transgressions, he was bruised for our iniquities: the chastisement of our peace was upon him; and with his stripes we are healed" (Isa 53:5).

- **Protection:** "LORD who shall abide in thy tabernacle? Who shall dwell in thy holy hill? He that walketh uprightly, and worketh righteousness, and speaketh the truth in his heart" (Ps 15:1–2).

- **Preservation:** "Thy LORD shall preserve thee from all evil: he shall preserve thy soul" (Ps 121:7).

- **Wholeness:** "The young lions do lack, and suffer hunger: but they that seek the LORD shall not want any good thing" (Ps 34:10).

- **Assurance:** "And this is the confidence that we have in him, that if we ask anything according to his will, he heareth us: And if we know that he hear us, whatsoever we ask, we know that we have the petitions that we desired of him" (1 Jn 5:14–15).

Bibliography

Carothers, Merlin. *Prison to Praise*. Escondido, California: Merlin Carothers, 2004.

Gravholt, Claus. 1996. Prenatal and postnatal prevalence of Turners Syndrome: A registry study. *BMJ* 312: 16–21.

Hook, E.B., and Warburton, D. 1983. The distribution of chromosomes/genotypes associated with Turner's Syndrome: Live birth prevalence rates and the evidence for diminished fetal mortality and severity in genotypes associated with structural X abnormalities or mosaicism. *Human Genetics* 64: 24–27.

Jacobs, P.A., and Hassold, T.J. 1995. The origin of numerical chromosome abnormalities. *Advanced Genetics* 33: 101–133.

Nee, Watchman. *Spiritual Reality or Obsession*. New York: Christian Fellowship PublishersInc., 1970.

Nee, Watchman. *Release of the Spirit*. Cloverdale, Indiana: Sure Foundation, 1965.

Rovet, Joanne. 1990. Turner Syndrome: Genetic and hormonal factors contributing to a specific learning disability profile. *Learning and Disabilities Research and Practice* 1930: 133–145.

Resources

Web site: knowledge2revelation.com

E-mail: georgecynthiaelias@knowledge2revelation.com
or georgecynthiaelias8@sympatico.ca

About the Author

Cynthia Elias is a petite, four-foot-eight visionary, whose knowledge and education took her through a master's in nursing from the University of South Carolina, MBA from Kennesaw University, and a doctorate and PhD in naturology from the American Institute of Holistic Theology. Cynthia's professional background includes a thirty-five-year career in the health care industry. During this time, she owned an assisted living complex for seniors. Cynthia transformed her focus of health care from a medical model to one of healthy living through the use of natural herbs and vitamins and, most importantly, the stripes of Jesus to heal.

For Cynthia, knowledge to revelation began as a breech birth. By the time she turned twelve, she appeared noticeably small in stature for her age. After numerous and embarrassing examinations at Johns Hopkins Hospital, the doctors diagnosed her with Turner syndrome. In many countries, when diagnosed in utero, the doctors abort these babies. How was this little girl going to survive in a world of perfection? With this concern etched in her mind, she set out to prove herself. God placed a special call on her life by giving her a brilliant mind, as seen through the pursuit of her education. During this time, she experienced two divorces, abuse, and many ungodly relationships. In addition, through a series of events, she lost her business. Cynthia rededicated her life to Christ and married a godly man. This is when the revelation and transformation of her life began and continues to be fulfilled.

The calling on her life now includes a healing ministry, life as a prophetess, and the heart to bless Israel. This powerful transformation and God's calling on their life brought Cynthia and her husband, George, to Ottawa, the gateway of Canada. They now live in Gatineau, Quebec, directly across the river from Ottawa. They have seven children living in Alberta, British Columbia, and Australia.

The book you hold is a testimony of the victory and power of Jesus to work in her life to overcome difficult circumstances. God has every individual destined for the same victory and power when one comes into a relationship with Jesus, taking one from a place of fear to freedom. One can then receive the revelation and calling for one's life by having a direct, intimate, and passionate relationship with God, Jesus, and the Holy Spirit.